AFTER MIDNIGHT

A Cressida Carlisle
Psychic Detective
Mystery

HF Dobson

Conspiracy of Ravens

CONSPIRACY OF RAVENS

First published in Australia in 2024 by Conspiracy of Ravens

ISBN 978-0-6459145-2-8 *(digital)*

ISBN 978-0-6459145-3-5 *(paperback)*

For JDF...

Something... just like this.

Without you, this wouldn't be possible xx

The *Cressida Carlisle* Catalogue —
the mystery history so far...

After Midnight

Beauty Sleep

Counting Sheep

Don't Let The Bedbugs Bite

Eine Kleine Nachtmusik (*coming soon!*)

Let's stay in touch!

Instagram @hfdobson

Facebook HF Dobson

Counting Crows

ONE for sorrow

TWO for mirth

THREE for a wedding

FOUR for a birth

FIVE for silver

SIX for gold

SEVEN a secret ne'er to be told

EIGHT for a wish

NINE for a kiss

TEN a bird you must not miss

ELEVEN for hope

TWELVE for health

THIRTEEN beware of the devil himself

Table of Contents

Friday 7.00pm...

When the going gets tough, the tough eat tiny sandwiches...

"Oh... *fuck!* Quick! Somebody grab this!"

Sorry. I do realise we're not getting off to the best of starts, however I have just stabbed a twenty-four gauge floristry wire into my index finger...and possibly right out the other side... can't be certain because I'm actually too scared to look.

And I have the more pressing problem that same hand is holding the bridal bouquet for tomorrow's Wedding of the Year - an obscene number of palest pink roses (Royal Highness, to be precise) expertly wired by yours truly into a work of art so epic it should be registered as a lethal weapon... and I am about to start pissing blood all over it.

My name is Cressida Carlisle and I'm a florist. I work at Melbourne's famous temple to the flower (and the *grand gesture...*) - Le Jardin. The public facade is a cool, calm haven of dark marble, mirrors and a breathtaking sea of flowers. The giant concrete bunker out the back is a somewhat different story, where a small, swearing army is charged with the very serious task of saying *Happy Birthday/Happy Baby/Happy New Year/Thank You!/Sorry You Died.../Sorry (for pretty much anything else)/Mazel Tov* on behalf of Melbourne's most Beautiful People.

On a good day, it's Well-Ordered Chaos.

Days like today, it is the fifth wheel of hell.

Our lovely bride is the only daughter of construction magnate - many would put inverted commas around that, because there have always been rumours about where Bruno Mancini's colossal fortune really comes from - who with a lot of charm and a lot of social media savvy has made herself a very bankable commodity in her own right.

The picture-perfect Angelica Mancini will be attended by fifteen bridesmaids, five flower girls, and will be celebrating her Special Day with almost a thousand of her closest friends. The five ring circus of a reception has one hundred tables.

That is a serious shitload of flowers, folks.

Which is why we're all still here at 7pm on a Friday night... and I'm supposed to be at a family dinner in thirty minutes, because tomorrow also happens to be my twenty-seventh Birthday.

The bouquet is whisked out of my hand by a junior minion and with a swift yank someone extracts the wire from my finger... which is when it starts thudding with pain... which is going to be all kinds of inconvenient, given the huge amount of work still to do tomorrow.

Said finger is wrapped like mummy in a bunch of those super ugly fabric Band Aids - because they're the only thing that stays on when you're battling wet foliage and plant slime.

Oh! It must be so lovely working here!

Yep. Lovely.

I add a few more roses... tweak a few this way or that... cast a critical eye over it... then pronounce it *Done!*

I stand in front of the full length mirror and hold it like the bride will tomorrow for the final once over...

Now... I could not possibly be more different from the super-model-like Insta Princess who'll be carrying it.

I am highly unremarkable.

Not particularly tall. Not especially short.

Not skinny, not fat.

Somewhere between ordinary and attractive, depending on time, motivation and level of effort.

My hair is longish and of indiscriminate colour too dark to be blonde and too light to be brunette. My skin turns a kind of attractive shade of gold with pretty minimal sun exposure (thank god - because I'm far too lazy to commit to fake tan...) The only interesting part is my eyes, which are green, and actually change colour with my level of self-care. After a big weekend, they glow like nuclear waste.

But I'm much happier talking about my work than myself...

And can I just say my bouquet is pretty freaking perfect.

Finally I can breathe out and smile.

I send a photo to Angelica's PA, then crop the shot down to a beautiful little sneak-peek detail for Le Jardin's socials (#lejardin #weddingbouquets #weddingsofmelbourne #idoidoido #prettiestinpink #guesswho #itsamelbournething)

"Divine darling! That is beyond divine!"

Our fearless leader, Troy James appears behind me in the mirror. Blond, tanned, glamorous and cheeky.

No one knows quite how old he is, but his appearance has remained unchanged for at least the last thirty years. He's hopeless with names. His solution - to what would be a considerable problem with a staff of over twenty - is to invent names for everyone.

I am Kitty-Kat.

I have no idea why...

He opens the door to the walk-in cool-room, pulling out a few bottles of Veuve Cliquot and a platter of tiny, fancy sandwiches.

Yep. I can feel a pep talk coming on...

"Okay Babes, let's call it a night. Thank you for today - I think we're on track. Get everything packed *carefully* - especially *that!* -" as he points at my bride's bouquet. "I need everyone working by seven tomorrow morning, yes? I'll be here thirty minutes before, with brekky arriving shortly after. It's going to be a massive day - there's a lot in the diary on top of the Mancini wedding... And this ridiculous weather won't help... But we'll get there! We always do... Grab a quick glass of bubbles, then get out of here!"

I order an Uber and send a quick text to Mum, snarling as the phone sits right on my war wound.

Just leaving now

Well... almost...

The junior minions distribute champagne in plastic cups and pass around the sandwiches.

I don't know whether it's the Army Marches On Its Stomach approach, or an acceptance that like toddlers we get very shitty kitty when hungry, but when the going gets tough here, the posh catering gets going.

A quick glance at my phone shows my Uber driver, Peter, is two minutes away.

I guzzle my champagne - because it'd be a crime to waste it - before saying my bye-byes and grabbing a sandwich (chicken breast, mayo & fresh herbs) for the road.

As I stand on the street eating my tasty sandwich, I realise I'm actually starving. Probably because I haven't eaten since noon. The heat of the day is radiating from the road, the footpath and the buildings surrounding me. The sky is still a clear, cloudless blue.

And there are ravens on the powerlines. Wall-to-wall ravens. Dozens and dozens of shiny, fat black bodies are gleaming in the golden, fading light.

"Seriously...?" I call up to them.

Seems like I've been seeing ravens everywhere these past few weeks. Ransacking the rubbish bins in the laneways behind work... sun baking on the balcony at home... playing King of the Castle on the gables of buildings... showing off hanging upside down from trees.

What's that nursery rhyme Gran used to sing about counting crows...? *One for sorrow, two for mirth...?*

"Haaa-haaa... Hrrrah!" one of them croaks and gurgles back at me.

"Sorry- I can't recall the rest, but I'm pretty sure it doesn't go up to fifty..." I laugh at him.

I vaguely remember ravens symbolised very different things in different ancient cultures, from harbingers of death to prophets of change and spiritual enlightenment, however I have absolutely no idea what it means to be stalked by them in 21st century Melbourne. If anything at all. Possibly it would be helpful if I could remember the goddam rhyme... *Three for a wedding, four for a birth...?* Hmmm... I stare up at them, wondering if their number is divisible by three... because it certainly *is* an exponentially epic wedding tomorrow. But just as I start counting them, my Uber pulls up, and my Raven Theory remains untested.

Friday 7:20 pm

A *Kerfuffle* of Family

"Hottest April day in history".

This is how Peter greets me. I raise a polite eyebrow to say *Really?*

He pushes his glasses up his nose in an irritated reflex action as he waits for a break in the traffic.

I don't know about *ever*... I certainly can't remember it being this hot on my Birthday before. However Peter is giving off the kind of Angry Middle-Aged White Man vibes that it's probably best just not to engage with him.

"You know it's all about the carbon, don't you...?"

I nod politely. Yes.

"And you know who's responsible for the carbon...?"

"We *all* are...?"

"*The Aliens!*"

Hmmm... not quite where I thought he was going with that...

"The Aliens are farming carbon!!!"

"*O-kay...*" I mouth silently, surreptitiously glancing down at my phone.

It should take about ten minutes to get from posh, leafy South Yarra to hip St Kilda on the bay, but with seemingly all of Melbourne out grabbing this last hurrah of Summer with both hands, the traffic is nuts. I resign myself to twenty-five minutes of smiling and nodding my way politely through hell.

The sun is slipping away and according to the dashboard, it's still a very Summery thirty degrees... when we should be sliding gently into Winter.

I'm wearing a black tank top, calf-length floaty black skirt, leopard print Birkenstocks and shiny tangerine toenails, thanks to a $20 Vietnamese pedicure last weekend.

You'll get used to the black.

It's a Melbourne thing.

I drag a brush through my hair, twisting it into a messy updo, then I fish a mirror out of my monster, kick-ass handbag - which was ridiculously expensive and I needed like a hole in the head, but being covered in suede, leather and patent fringe in every shade of purple, it so reminded me of an exotic bird there was no way I was leaving without it. As Simon says, you only regret what you don't buy - and we'll get to him later.

Yep.

Little mirror shows I look as sweaty and exhausted as a I feel. I reach for the sparkly pinky-nude lip gloss, in the vain hope that it'll chirp me up a bit.

Finally we pull up out the front of The Beach House, perched in prime position right on the promenade. The sea of beautiful people waiting for a table has spilled out of the bar and onto the sidewalk.

There's a lot of tanned skin, great hair and perfect 'no makeup' makeup. Bare shoulders, bare legs. Some of the guys have broken out the hipster shorts.

Beneath the clatter of people eating, laughing and having a good time, there's the funky sax and bass notes of acid jazz. I wriggle my way through the crowd, give the bar staff a little wave and head to the private dining room. The Beach House has been our Special Dinner go-to restaurant forever, so I'm trying not to sound like one of *those* people, but they know us here.

There's an ornate peek-a-boo carved screen next to the doorway, which allows the waiting staff to keep an eye on the table without having to interrupt the room. I pause for a moment to watch my family in action before throwing myself into it.

I can't help but smile and my heart swells.

Dad is at the head of the table, in his element.

Holding court. Telling a funny story.

His eyes twinkling and his hands waving wildly. My mother sits on his left, monitoring the perilous trajectory of his gesturing in relation to the glassware on the table...

My Dad tells stories for a living.

As one of Melbourne's most prominent barristers, he gets paid hundreds an hour to tell stories.

I'll wait for him to finish... I don't want to steal his thunder.

At his left hand - like a Queen - is my Mum.

Jane Carlisle is generally described as either magnificent or terrifying.

Tall, handsome, golden.

Glamorous. Beautifully preserved. Perfectly maintained.

That her very British Home Counties accent hasn't slipped an inch - despite living here for over thirty years - further ups her intimidation factor.

We call her TBJ - The Beautiful Janey.

Next to her is Miranda, my five-years older sister.

Pretty much a mini-me of Mum, but a little taller and a lot less prickly. Good at everything.

Smart. Sporty. School Captain.

Graduated Law at Melbourne with Honours and now is the third generation of proud Carlisles to practice in the family business. (I was supposed to be a member of that club too... But that's another story for another day...)

And she's about to add Model Mother to her resume. (And I mean 'about' quite literally. She's due to drop it any day now...) Even at the end of her Yummy-Mummy-Pilates-Organic pregnancy she barely looks any different. A silk chiffon Kaftan skims her gently swollen breasts and tasteful baby bump.

Next to Miranda is her husband, Marc. He sometimes gets Marco - the name his Very Italian parents gave him.

Yep. The crazy curly hair and the kooky glasses give the game away.

Marc is an architect. An architect who gets paid a lot of money for his 'revolutionary' designs - often by evil property developers. Marc placates his conscience by designing affordable housing that can be made from plastic milk bottles in his spare time.

Or something like that...

The empty seat on Dad's right is for The Birthday Girl.

Next to that... my grandparents.

Grandpa is - you guessed it - a lawyer, and founder of Carlisle & Carlisle. If my Dad is the typical jovial Delinquent Scotsman, Grandpa is the typical Dour One. Imposingly tall and unfailingly dignified. He generally chooses to listen rather than talk, but when he speaks, you need to be all ears. It will either be mind altering wisdom... or the darkest, funniest thing you have ever heard in your life.

Despite the big retirement party over ten years ago, he still puts on his collar'n'tie and goes into the office pretty much every day.

Okay.

Gran...

Gran is one of my favourite people on the planet.

She will not go quietly into old age, still dying her wavy hair a brilliant auburn. Her groovy, oversize glasses make her green eyes even more hypnotic. Everyone always says I'm most like Gran... Even though she's pale and petite, we have the curves, the

14

green eyes... and a not quite *normal* way of seeing things in common.

She's actually psychic.

Yes. I kid you not.

She.

Is.

Psychic.

Like the police call her when they need help. Like she has celebrities numbers in her phone - not that she would *ever* talk about that.

She once had very high hopes for me.

When I was little, I'd often find people to chat with... who nobody else in the room could see. As you can imagine, TBJ was *horrified* by this and actively discouraged the making of new friends with dead people. Which Gran declared a 'terrible, terrible waste' (roll your R's when you say that. Gran is also a Scot).

I guess she's never given up hope that one day my 'gift' will come back...

And the last seat - with its' back to me - is Larry.

Larry is my five-years-younger sister.

Yes.

Sister.

Larry was really supposed to be a boy, so TBJ decided that giving 'him' my grandfather's name - Laurence - in utero would make that happen. But like most mothers, Mother Nature doesn't like to be told what to do...

The name is the only masculine thing about Larry. She is all pint-sized dangerous curves and she is crafty (and I don't mean as in glitter/fabric glue/egg cartons. I'm talking sneaky...)

From the second she realised her enormous big blue eyes could make pretty much anyone do pretty much anything, Miranda and I have been covering for her.

She is sweet, flippant, feel-good chaos for whom the Rules have never been more than an inconvenient suggestion.

The table erupts into laughter.... which is my cue to enter.

"Here's Trouble!" Dad beams at me... a little louder and a little more jovial than usual. Which would suggest that the almost-empty high ball glass in front of him was not his first Hendricks and tonic of the evening...

The nick-name predates memory... no idea how I got saddled with it... sometimes things do not have a necessarily *straight forward* outcome once I become involved... however in my defence,

16

the consummately perfect Miranda was always going to be a hard act to follow. And if they thought I was *challenging*, nothing was going to prepare them for Larry...

"Hey! Sorry I'm late... Oh please don't get up!"

I do a quick lap of the table, planting smooches on everyone's cheeks before they can start pushing their chairs back to stand.

When I get to TBJ, she looks at me imploringly, yet faintly hopeful.

"No Simon...?"

"He's working... a music video or something. They're shooting on the beach just 'round in Port Melbourne - he said might get here in time for cake if they wrap early enough. He sends his love."

A collective *Ah!* from the table.

Everyone loves Simon. We live together.

Don't get excited - not like *that*.

Simon - as Gran would say - bats for the other team.

Simon is a fashion stylist. His innate ability to make people feel good about themselves (as well as look a million dollars) keeps him constantly in demand. He is also my Bestie.

Then TBJ zeroes in on my finger.

"Oh my God! What have you done to yourself?! Did you put Dettol on that? Have you had a tetanus shot?"

I lie and nod a vague Yes in answer to all the questions.

She raises a suspicious eyebrow at me. There's no fooling TBJ. And then her lovely brow furrows. She's appraising the rest of my hands. Florist's Hands. No nails... covered in cuts, scratches and pollen stains... and random, angry red bumps that are probably harbouring rose thorns. She shakes her head whilst muttering *Oh dear!* under her breath, as she reaches for her champagne.

I collapse into my seat as Dad hands me a tall glass that clinks with ice and smells promisingly of sharp bittersweet botanicals and fresh citrus.

"A Tom Collins for the Birthday Girl...?"

"Oh good God yes!"

One giant slurp and I'm instantly feeling cooler and calmer. I realise this would most likely get me points on the AA quiz... I start recounting my Uber experience.

"Oh you got Conspiracy Pete!" Larry laughs, big blue eyes twinkling. "He's freaking hi-*lar*-ious! Wait til you hear the one about stolen children the government's hiding in the tunnels under the river..."

We do a collective partially disbelieving frown and head shake.

"Hey - has anyone else noticed the ravens...? They're everywhere! There was a herd of like *fifty* on the powerlines outside work."

"It's actually a *rave*" says Larry with great authority as she drains her martini glass.

"Sorry...?"

A quick glance around the table confirms I'm not the only one who's confused.

"A rave of ravens. Or a *treachery*... Or an *unkindness*. Or..." she pauses for dramatic impact "... a *conspiracy* - which is my personal favourite."

We're all staring at her, astonished and somewhat skeptical but nonetheless impressed.

"What...?" as she looks around for a waiter to bring her another drink. "I love a good collective noun. Doesn't everyone...?"

Oh I should ask Gran for a Counting Crows refresher... but before I can, she clasps her hand over mine and squeezes it. I can feel her emotion.

"Oh! Ravens! Excellent!"

Everyone starts looking a little uncomfortable. There's a very good chance Gran is about to go weird on us.

"Darling girl! The ravens are a sign. Your Return of Saturn - it's early... and it's tonight! Just after midnight! Oh think what it might bring...!"

Everyone at the table rolls their eyes and reaches for their glass. Except Marco.

"What's a Return of Saturn...?"

"Astrology - " explains Miranda, with a mouthful of sourdough bread, talking in a flat, matter-of-fact tone. Like someone bringing you up to speed with a soap opera.

"Every 27 to 29 years Saturn returns to where it was in the sky when you were born. Saturn is the cosmic taskmaster - challenges, strength, wisdom, obstacles yada-yada... It represents what's important - or *should be* important - to you... goals, values... and forces change to bring you into alignment with your true path..."

"The short answer...?" interjects a very smug Larry. "Shit is about to get real for Sid."

Marco nods slowly. Like the rest of us, he's learnt that even if it sounds completely like witchcraft, examples can usually be provided to suggest that it could possibly be a thing.

"So this happens tonight...? After midnight??? When exactly *after midnight*??? Is it like tick... tick... tick...*BOOM!*...???" Marco asks, with clearly more questions presenting themself by the second. His architect's brain is hardwired to rationalise and iron out details.

"The planet moves just after midnight. The effect could be instantaneous... it could take months... years even... and it may be multi-faceted..." is Gran's expansive, yet evasive reply.

Marco, unable to leave Well Enough alone, keeps unpacking it.

"So... Miranda's Return of Saturn would have been when she finally agreed to go out with me...?"

"Yes!" Gran beams. And nods knowingly. "Yes it was! All she did was work, work, work... then she finally noticed you! A beautiful couple... soon to have a beautiful little girl... A balanced life! Her true path! "

"How do you know it's a girl? We didn't find out..."

Gran raises an eyebrow and tries not to look smug.

"It'd better be a girl." TBJ pipes up. " Little boys are no fun at all to shop for..."

Larry slaps her hand over her mouth, making spluttering noises as she struggles to manage simultaneously laughing hysterically and swallowing a mouthful of watermelon pink rocket fuel.

"So is Sid about to... get married and... *have babies...?*"

Everyone turns their attention to me... I know they're all hoping my True Path will have nothing to do with Playing House... rather it will involve growing up, giving up playing with flowers, completing a law degree and pulling my weight in the family business.

Being Responsible.

"Just so long as you don't start... you know... *talking with invisible people* again..." Miranda pulls a face, shuddering. "That was profoundly disturbing."

Can't help it. I giggle because being able to chat with ghosts was actually pretty cool and kinda funny from where I was standing. And being able to scare the crap out of your big sister was highly entertaining.

I don't have to look to know Gran's smile has widened.

That is *exactly* what she is hoping will happen.

And I hate to tell her, but it's massively unlikely. I lost that ability years ago. The best I can do now is the occasional freak out when I walk into a room where something bad has happened, and the odd deja vu.

And as for that Other purpose... I'm pretty sure I don't need one, Saturn. I'm good, thanks! I'm actually quite happy with my life the way it is. I guess I wouldn't mind a 'someone' in it... however I have no desire to 'adult'. And I've honestly no idea how to go about that. I count relationships in weeks, not even months... let alone years. I like short term, instant gratification, zero ramifications - both personally and professionally. Smashing out pretty floral arrangements all day is without complication. The weight of consequence, and the greater weight of conscience - never mind the power suits, intimidating shoes and necessity of daily pantyhose - are all baggage that come with practicing law... And burdens I have absolutely no intention of carrying.

So with all respect to the zodiac, I really can't see how what a planet does after midnight can change that.

Come on down, Saturn... Hit me with your best shot!

A waiter appears and asks if we're ready to order.

"Oh good God yes!" TBJ is so relieved to change the subject the words are out of her mouth before she can stop them. She waves a graceful, French manicured hand over the table.

"Just bring out platters of whatever's good tonight please, Tyler. Oh! And don't forget we have a pregnant lady!"

Can I just say the list of things that Miranda has obsessively avoided for the past nine months is enough to make me never want children...

Then she turns her attention to me.

"So... the Big Day tomorrow... What's Princess Angelica wearing? What colour are the bridesmaids? I heard she's having twenty! Is she really having twenty...??? How big is the reception, because quite frankly I don't know anyone who *isn't* invited..."

I press my lips together and shake my head.

"Client privilege. I say nothing!!!"

"I was unaware florists took an oath."

"Oh... we know everyone's secrets before the world'n'his wife finds out. Affairs, engagements, babies... illnesses. *And we don't tell.* Because it's kinda bad for business..."

24

"Bah! You're no fun at all. I must say I'm extremely unhappy about the weather - " like it is somehow Angelica's's fault. "God knows what I'm going to wear. When one buys an outfit for an April wedding one isn't expecting thirty bloody degrees..."

"She's such a pretty girl she'd look great in anything."Miranda enthuses. Kind. Magnanimous. Genuine.

"We work with her a lot. She's gorgeous." I cannot lie. Despite being everything that really should make my eye twitch, she *is* gorgeous.

Lovely Larry at the end of the table pulls a very un-lovely face.

"D'ya think...? I think she's very basic. And boring. And predictable. *And* she's freaking illiterate! How can one not know the difference between a plural and a possessive...?"

The whole table turns in surprise to consider Larry's seemingly disproportionate amount of anger at the inappropriate use of an apostrophe... which really doesn't make sense.

And neither does the very uncharacteristic baggy floral dress she's wearing. Her style is usually Maximum Effect, not Little House on the Prairie.

However Larry is saved from cross-examination by the arrival of food. Gigantic, stylish, white oval platters of everything you want to eat on a beautiful, balmy night.

Kingfish ceviche... char-grilled calamari... Greek-style lamb... tomato and mozzarella salad... perfectly dressed leafy greens... crispy roasted potatoes...

Food is passed around the table, wine is ordered, glasses are filled...and the conversation gets quick-fire and rowdy. With so many lively minds, quick wits and sharp tongues, it's a verbal amusement park.

Roller coaster... dodgem cars... merry-go-round...

Personal lives... Politics... Headlines...

It twists, turns, jumps, slams, and every so often plummets. There's a lot of laughter - and the occasional scream - as we get progressively louder and louder.

The platters are cleared and a spectacular Birthday cake appears.

Mmmm... chocolate!

Tyler, our waiter, offers to take a photo. We all smile for the smartphone, then they sing Happy Birthday to me... after which TBJ presents me with an envelope.

"Right!" She says briskly and emphatically. This generally precedes something not pleasant... like *Clean your room* or *You have a dental appointment on Thursday*... "Darling, you're twenty-seven. Like it or not, you're a Grown Up now..."

Nope. Grown up is something I quite specifically do not want to be. I regard the envelope suspiciously. What the hell has she put in there...?

"Maybe you could try looking after yourself, Darling... Just a little bit...? I know that Minimal Caring look is fashionable, but you do need to start thinking about how you're going to weather the storm..."

And realising I have no intention of opening Pandora's Envelope, pulls out a card from Entre Nous Day Spa with a list of monthly dates for a year. The first being this coming Tuesday...

"We all chipped in... It's a year of appointments with Holly... She's a *magician*. Simon is booked in too - that way I know you'll be made to go..."

Well... I've never really had enough time to be High Mainte-nance... and I've always kinda had better things to do... The ap-pointment thing is a challenge, because both work and my extra-curricular activities (especially with Simon as my Social Secretary) have a tendency to spiral out of control. So given I'm already fail-ing maintenance, *preventible* is clearly going to be a stretch...

Well-played TBJ for thinking to schedule it with Simon...

Well-played...

We all eat cake. Except for Larry, which is odd because she's usually the most indulgent (and least wary of consequence) at the table.

And she keeps sneaking surreptitious glances at her phone. Now Laurence Carlisle Senior is Old School and has a very strict dining etiquette rule - first person to touch their phone pays the bill. She's so dying to text her thumbs are veritably twitching, but she also knows she doesn't have how ever many hundred dollars we've run up. And she's really *not* the type to do the dishes.

As we push our chairs back to say our goodbyes, Gran pats my hand.

28

"Is it your day off on Tuesday, dear...? You still haven't met Michael... he's such a lovely young man. Come for lunch - I'll see if he's free to join us... Bring Simon..."

And oh God! Here we go again.

Gran's been trying forever to get me and her Lovely Young Man in the same room. All I know is he's a country boy and that he's 'lovely'.

Seriously, Gran...? I can't see me having *anything* in common with either Country or Lovely. I smile and nod vaguely, but my eyes say *Yeah-Nah* - which is Australian for *that is a really bad idea and it's not happening.*

Designated drivers Miranda and TBJ start rattling their car keys.

"Sid, we can give you a ride home. We've got Gran and Grandpa, but there's room for one more."

Larry pipes up.

"Oh, I thought Sid could share an Uber with me. I've got a debating club meeting just around the corner from her..."

TBJ narrows her eyes. The frump dress and clock-watching hasn't gone unnoticed by her either.

"Isn't it a little late for a meeting...?"

"Oh no. Not at all." Smoothly. All big blue-eyed innocence. "A few of the guys had to work tonight."

"Work!" exclaims Dad, delighting in the irony. "Imagine that...!"

"Rude! I tried to work for you and you sacked me!" That very pretty face can also do a very convincing Pouty And Indignant.

"You went out to get morning coffee and you never came back. You lasted precisely fifty-three minutes..."

"Maybe Cressida could get you something at Le Jardin...?" TBJ's voice is bright and hopeful..

Oh Good God no!

After a second of wide-eyed deer-caught-in-headlights panic, I manage an almost smooth reply...

"I don't think we have anything... suitable... I love her, but I'd say she's more of a You problem, than a Me problem..."

Mum and Dad recently sold the house we grew up in, buying a very glamorous city apartment in the hope of being Empty Nest-ers. Unfortunately Larry is far too lazy and too smart to fly the coop - especially when the new nest is minutes from Melbourne University (...where, yes, you guessed it... she's doing Law.) So I'm guessing Larry isn't going to stop being a Them Problem any time soon.

We all make our way out through the packed, partying bar and spill out into the uncharacteristically balmy night. Big hugs and smoochie kisses all round as we say our goodbyes.

Dad holds me close, giving me one last extra-tight squeeze, then holds me out at arm's length.

"Ah... Trouble! Look at you! Twenty-seven!!! Where did it go...?" he shakes his head wistfully, then his hand motions almost imperceptibly to his pocket. "Are you okay? Do you need- "

"Thank you, but I'm fine. I don't need money. My rent is crazy-cheap, and Simon's always bringing home free stuff..."

He smiles at me, bemused, as Not Needing Money is quite a foreign concept to the other women in his life.

"Laurence..." he turns to farewell Larry.

Her eyes widen hopefully. She's always very happy to take his money.

"Behave yourself!"

And with a theatrical little bow, he turns and disappears into the night.

And then it's just me and Larry waiting for our ride.

And a raven, head-down bum-up, fishing for snacks in the rubbish bin. *One for sorrow*, right...???

"How's Uni...?" I ask. "How're you liking second year?"

She gives little snort, screwing up her pretty nose.

She struggled to get into Law - due more to her attitude than her ability - and I can't help but wonder if she really wants to be there. And I'd be the last person to blame her. Slowly and thought-fully she turns to look at me.

"Do you miss it...?"

I give a shrug.

"I guess I miss using my brain that way... I miss the reading and the problem solving. I don't miss the game-playing and the politics and the wankers."

"Would you like to use your brain to write a paper for me...?" Larry asks sweetly.

I laugh out loud.

"No! No I would most certainly *not* like to write a paper for you! When's it due?"

An exasperated snort.

"Today."

"*Larry!*" in the Universal Big Sister Voice that combines horror, disappointment and admonishment.

Another exasperated snort, accompanied by a theatrical toss of her glossy and expensive ombre locks that shade from golden brown to blonde, is interrupted by the arrival of our car. Just as I'm waving *over here* to our driver on the other side of the street, a shock of panic jolts every fibre of my being.

LARRY!

Something is about to happen to Larry...

And before I can dismiss this as ridiculous, she's stepping off the curb... and from out of nowhere an engine roars, headlights blind me and I'm reaching out to grab her arm. Her name is coming out of my mouth in a bloodcurdling, panic-stricken scream. My fingers close around her wrist and I yank her backwards with all my might. A nanosecond later a car speeds through the spot where she was standing. In my head, I can see it ploughing into her then sucking her crumpled body underneath...

"*You fucking idiot!*" Lovely Larry screams after the driver.

No need to ask her if she's okay...

My pulse is still thudding in my ears as I cross the street and my hand is shaking as I open the car door and collapse into the back seat.

We slip out of St Kilda, where the streets are still packed with people obviously up for a big Friday night. I watch a little too intently out the window.

I have no idea what to say.

I have no idea what to think.

Did I seriously just have a Psychic Moment...?

Suddenly I sense her wriggling and shimmying in her seat.

"What *are* you doing???"

She has almost managed to remove the frumpy floral dress, revealing a sexy little halter top, some dangerously short shorts and a *lot* of smooth, golden skin.

Our driver is also watching the show in his rearview mirror.

"Nothing..." is her evasive reply, as she fishes makeup from her handbag and starts working on her lips with the kind of precision reserved for when you really want to make someone want to kiss them.

"And what's *that*???"

I point at the laurel wreath tattoo curling delicately around her shoulder blade.

"Is that new? Does Mum know???"

"Yes and no. And she's not going to find out, *is she???*"

Oh, she'll find out alright. Her ability to find things out is so prodigious it's disturbing. Whenever Dad thinks he's missing something in a case and the Private Investigators turn up nothing, he gets TBJ on the job. Three letters - like KGB or CIA - and that is no coincidence.

Her phone buzzes inside her handbag. She pounces, simultaneously fishing it out, reading and replying.

Urgently.

"Cute phone case. Is that new...?" Clearly if she's being all Secret Squirrel, there's no point asking *who*... so I try deflecting. And can I just say... it *is* cute as a button. Baby pink with sprinkles of sparkly little jewels and a big LC monogram. Not my style, but it's perfectly Larry.

She looks up, clearly happy to steer the conversation away from other inconvenient questions.

"I won it in a competition... that I don't even remember entering... How funny is that??? It just arrived in the mail one day last week..."

How typical is that...? Welcome to the charmed existence of Lovely Larry!

I'm almost home. I live not far from work. A ten minute walk if I'm daydreaming, five if I'm motivated. I don't have a car because I really don't need one. (Flatmate Simon would possibly argue to the contrary...)

We pull up out the front of my grand Art Deco building. Our driver looks at Larry when it becomes obvious that I'm the only one getting out.

"Where to for you?"

I'm about to open the door, but I pause, waiting for her answer.

"*Bye bye!*" she says loudly and pointedly.

"Rude!" I laugh in mock offence as I open the door.

Then I get a pang of conscience. She may be up to something, but she's still my baby sister.

Who just had a near-death experience...

"Hey! Take care... Love you like a rainbow!"

She's in the shadows, but I can see her face soften.

"Yeah... Ditto..."

(Almost) After Midnight

I climb the stairs to the fourth floor. There are eight apartments. Two on each floor - one to the left and one to the right with a communal staircase up the middle. It's old school - no foyer, no security. Each landing is open to the street below.

I guess I should feel anxious walking up in the dark by myself, but there's really nothing shady or dangerous about South Yarra.

I turn my key and open the door to darkness.

No Simon yet.

It's beautiful to look at - original parquetry floors, period details, lots of light and views of leafy old trees along the river bank, with a glimpse of the city lights on the other side.

It's not so beautiful to live in.

The basic white tiled kitchen and bathroom are tiny and archaic. It's hot in Summer and freezing in Winter. Right now it's stuffy and oppressive. And I'm too scared to open windows because the freaking mosquitoes will eat me alive.

I dump my bag in the living room, and with a yawn glance at the clock on the mantelpiece.

Almost midnight.

Could be better, could be worse...

A message buzzes on my phone.

(SIMON) Party on the beach with Seven!

Get here right now!!!

(ME) No can do

Big day tomo - need Zzzzzzz

I sigh. So I have just chosen Sensible over meeting the Sexiest Man Alive (aka Tom Hardy, Seven's lead singer)... This birthday is truly getting off to a flying start... *NOT!*

Frowning, I set an alarm on my phone for 5.45 am, resolutely placing it on my bedside table. Resisting the urge to look at it.

I need sleep. Now.

Tomorrow is going to be so massive it doesn't bear thinking about.

I turn on the electric fan at the end of my bed, cranking it up to hurricane speed. Fortunately I'm good at sleeping - Miranda, Larry and I all are. TBJ takes full credit for 'training us' as babies.

Her method involved a large dose of Phenergan and a big splash of Dad's single malt in our bottles. It's possibly not to be recommended, but I will point out we all turned out okay - and we can fall asleep pretty much anywhere.

I pull the sheet over me - it's too hot for anything else - and let my head fall into my pillow. I vaguely wonder about what Gran said... the Saturn Thing... what might it be up to?... when does it actually make it's move?... how will I even know? ...as I wait for sleep to find me...

Isn't it funny how you never know the exact moment that sleep...

finds...

you...

hmmm...

funny...

There's a girl sitting on an expensive, modern black leather sofa pulling on bright red running shoes. She stands up and pulls her long, straight, shiny black hair into a ponytail.

She's Asian... Chinese, maybe?

She's wearing a loose, black tank top over a black crop sports bra and spandex running shorts. She's lean and fit.

"Hey I can't sleep - I'm going for a run," she calls out to her sister in another room.

"Really?!" a surprised voice floats back. "It's after midnight!"

"It's okay. I'll take Bear with me."

No. No. Please don't do it.

She clips the lead onto a Golden Retriever and heads out into the hallway. We're in a luxury modern apartment building. She stretches her quads and hamstrings while she waits for the lift.

She does more stretching on the way down, then we're out on the sidewalk in the still-warm night air.

Turn around. Go back!

I don't know how, but I know that something very bad is about to happen.

She stuffs earbuds into her ears, taps her Apple Watch a few times and the music starts...

A chirpy guitar riff.. some punchy drums... some soulful wailing...

Involuntarily I grin.

With the uncool guilty-pleasure anthem, MMMBop, ringing in our ears, we take off like gazelles and start running through the streets of Melbourne.

She mutters the lyrics under her breath as she powers along.

And somehow I can keep up with her.

Somehow I can run.

Which is amazing because one thing I have never been is fit.

It is exhilarating. I feel so strong and powerful, rhythmically pulling air in through my nose to inflate my lungs, then letting it go as my arms swing in time and my legs propel me along at incredible speed.

But I also feel my unease growing.

Then I'm aware of the white van.

And unease gives way to dread.

Turn around. Go home. Please go home!

But she keeps on running.

We're in the business end of town now. Tall skyscrapers line empty streets.

There's no traffic. No people.

Just the white van.

She thinks about turning for home, deliberating between the shortcut up the service laneways or the long way round. She feels Bear is flagging a little.

No! Please no. Not the lane...

She turns up the laneway.

She doesn't hear the van speed off.

She doesn't notice the van slowly reappear at the end of the lane.

Turn around. Oh God! Turn around!

Dread gives way to panic. I try to scream at her, but nothing comes out of my mouth.

She looks down to check her watch.

She doesn't see them appear, but she feels Bear's growling reverberate up the lead. She looks up, but it's too late.

They grab her.

She fights.

She tries to kick them but three big men quickly and efficiently overpower her.

Bear lunges, grabbing one of them on the arm. He is frantic, trying to protect her. One of them kicks him with full force.

44

There's a sickening, cracking noise. Bear collapses. She is terrified for herself and desperate for her dog.

One of them clamps a cloth over her nose.

It smells chemical - like disinfectant.

There's a sweet taste in her mouth. And she folds like a rag doll.

One of them whisks her into the van while the other two pick up Bear and with difficulty lob his limp body into a dumpster.

I stand there, sickened and helpless.

Hearing the doors slam shut.

Watching the van speed away.

She is lying on a narrow bed in a tiny room.

There's a basic toilet and tiny sink, like a prison cell. There are no windows. She is still unconscious. He sits at the foot of the bed. Hovering over her like she's his prize.

He speaks softly. Slowly. Deliberately. His voice is heavy with an Eastern European accent that I can't quite place.

They have removed her clothes. She is wearing a white terry bathrobe. An iron manacle lined with sheepskin has been clamped around her wrist. She is chained to the wall.

I am so fearful for her I can't breathe.

I hear my heartbeat pounding in my head.

There is nothing I can do.

One of the men who stalked her watches from the doorway. He is cautious, slightly anxious.

"You have outdone yourself. This one pleases me very much. A little China Doll for my collection."

He runs a finger down her smooth, pale leg. He pauses at the indentation left from her socks at her ankle. The imperfection is distasteful to him.

"Tomorrow night we shall have a date. Make the necessary preparations."

He leaves the room.

The door closes and three bolts slide into place with three ominous thunks.

Rising under sufferance. Shining highly unlikely.

"Hey Sid... Sid!...*Cressida!*

The voice is coming from a long way away. There's a very irritating faint ringing and beeping too. And I want it all to go away. I'm floating somewhere soft, peaceful and empty.

I like it here.

Hands grip my arms and shake me.

"*Cressida!... Wake up!... Wake up!*"

And I'm dragged back.

I'm lying in a sweat-soaked bed.

Slowly I open my eyes.

Bright blue eyes looking very concerned and fluffy yellow-blond hair like a baby chicken.

Simon.

I blink vaguely at him.

"*It's seven thirty!!!*"

Hmmm...

Wheels slowly starting to turn...

And then the brain kicks into gear.

"*Oh fuck!*"

I fling myself out of bed and almost pitch headlong into the floor.

My head is spinning. My heart is lurching like I'm on a roller-coaster. My stomach is convulsing and I feel like I'm sweating from every pore.

Simon is throwing clothes at me. This is when your best friend who gets paid to dress women for a living becomes a friend with a very different kind of benefit... Black t-shirt bra... black comfy knickers... black tank top... stretchy, skinny olive cargo pants...

Cargo pants...? Freaking excellent!... Yep. It's going to be a cargo pants kind of day.

And I'm seriously late for it.

I grab my phone. Eleven missed calls from work and the alarm still bleating. I stuff my feet into my Birkenstocks and moving as fast as my wobbly legs will permit, snatch my handbag from the living room and head to the front door. Simon is already there, holding his car keys. Bless!

He runs, I stagger down the stairs.

My phone rings again.

Uh-oh. It's Troy.

"Alarm didn't go off... I am so sorry..."

It's difficult to get the words out, pitching myself unsteadily down three flights with waves of nausea crashing over me.

"I'm two minutes away."

On the other end there's a pause. Relief that I've finally surfaced giving way to pissed off that I'm not already there.

"Go straight to the car park - the vans are just about loaded. Drop off the groom's flowers on the way to the hotel for the bride. She's expecting you at eight."

Troy's smart enough to know there's too much to be done today to bang on about my lateness.

He's about to hang up, but he hesitates.

"Is everything okay? This isn't like you at all..."

"Yep. All good." I puff through clenched teeth, as I yank the door open to Simon's white baby Range Rover.

Collapsing into the passenger seat I close my eyes and try to get my body under some kind of control. I don't know what the hell is going on.

The dream...

What the hell was that dream...???

And why do I feel like I've lived it...?

Breathe in two... three...

And out... two... three... (which isn't easy when Simon is re-enacting the car chase from Ronin.)

I can't get the dream out of my head... Every detail is agonisingly clear. I keep seeing her face. Feeling her terror.

Babe! Pull it together!

"If you need a ride home, just yell..." Simon looks really worried as he pulls into the car park. The best I can mange is a vague nod.

A junior minion sees me and points out one of the fleet of dark green Le Jardin delivery vans. I'm incredibly relieved to be able to slip out before anyone can see me.

Or smell me.

I feel hot, sweaty and revolting. And I'm so exhausted I feel physically ill.

I turn the key in the ignition and Metallica blasts from the speakers...

Dude, at this point I'm too scared to close either eye ever again.

I head towards Docklands, skirting the edge of the city. I'm hoping it'll take less than ten minutes. I really don't like playing catch up.

I become aware that the index finger of my left hand is throbbing as I notice the somewhat unhygienic-looking Bandaids from yesterday still wrapped around it.

Oh great!

And the hits just keep coming...

I may be running late, but at least I'm still too early for Saturday morning traffic. In no time at all I'm pulling into the underground service carpark of Melbourne's most extravagant residential tower, Stratus.

Security gives me a nod and waves me through. I swear a Le Jardin van could get you into pretty much anywhere, no questions asked.

I pull on my dark green Le Jardin apron, grabbing the box of buttonholes - or boutonnières if you want to be posh about it - for the groom and his fifteen groomsmen. Each one a chic, simple pale pink rose - same as the bride's bouquet.

The building, like mine, has two apartments on each floor. But that's where the similarities end. The lower floors house necessary amenities - parking, storage, gym - and 'necessary' amenities - concierge, personal shopper, pool, wellness centre, board rooms, private dining rooms. The upper levels house the A List. Every palatial floor has sweeping views out to Port Phillip bay on one side, and back over to the city skyline from the other.

Glass, marble.

Immaculate, expensive.

The list of residents is a who's who. If you live in this building, there's a good chance I know a disturbing amount about your personal life because I'm either delivering to you, or sending flowers for you on a very regular basis.

The concierge in the foyer calls up to the penthouse for me.

I can't avoid the mirrors in the lift.

I don't think it's possible to feel worse physically or mentally after my Nightmare Episode. A glance at my reflection confirms I look every bit as bad as all that. Puffy, blotchy, sweaty.

With my one free hand I quickly try to smooth my hair and wipe away yesterday's mascara from under my eyes.

Ding!

It's Simon.

R u ok?

I send back a thumbs up Emoji.

And the green-face-supressing-vomit one...

Ping! The doors open and I'm face to face with

Larry...?!

An extremely dishevelled Larry.

What the...???

She falters for a split second, then says smoothy -

"We ended up here. It got so late we all just crashed...." as she gestures vaguely to one of the doors.

Now this would probably have flown with anyone else, however I happen to know that apartment belongs to Maude Mason, the eccentric seventy year old fashion designer.... so either Maude's making a late start on a law degree and has enrolled as an *extremely* mature age student...

Or somebody's lying.

I just raise an eyebrow (TBJ style), but before I can think of something to say, Door Number Two opens and a smooth voice calls out... *Hey!*

Larry turns, as a baby pink tulle Cosabella g-string is catapulted through the air, and lands in her cleavage. Our groom is standing the doorway, wearing a pair of jeans.

Yep.

Just a pair of jeans.

Ash Knight is more attractive than anyone really has a right to be. Aussie dad, Indian mum. Tall, dark, smooth and ridiculously Bollywood hero handsome. He turned one hip Indian-fusion restaurant into a stable of bankable bars and eateries, however when you look like *that*, the jump to celebrity chef wasn't hard.

Actually, it was inevitable..

"Oh Cressida! Come on through..."

He winks at Larry, then turns on his bare feet leaving the door ajar behind him. It registers vaguely that even his feet are smooth and sexy.

I shake my head like a dog trying to get water out of its ears. After my ordeal last night, this is more weird and wrong than I can even begin to process.

Larry decides attack is the best defence and comes out swinging.

"You look like hell!"

Rude, but there's actually no arguing with that.

I shake my head again, trying to unsee my baby sister's knickers flying through the air, but I don't think that will ever happen.

She has to walk past me to get into the lift.

"Your dress is inside out!" I retort, quietly yet pointedly.

Touche, Chickenhead.

I enter the cool, beautiful apartment. He is fortunately nowhere to be seen.

My struggle with the supreme awkwardness of the situation is interrupted and a little placated by a vague, random realisation.

He doesn't know that she's your sister, right...? Why would he...???

His smooth voice calls out -

"You can just leave them on the dining table, Cressida... Thank you!"

Suits me just fine, thank you.

Now. This is when I realise that I haven't been to the loo, and that jittery feeling in my belly is rapidly giving way to panic. It is highly unprofessional - and more than a little embarrassing - but given I don't have to do it face to face, I hesitantly call out -

"Hey, may I use your bathroom?"

"Of course. The door on the right in the entrance foyer."

It's all smooth, tobacco brown marble - serene, dark and radiating cool. I lean sideways, resting my cheek on the wall. I slip my feet out of my Birkenstocks and press them into the floor.

Ah, that's better.

You know... I'd really like to lie down on the cool, smooth floor and pretend that today isn't happening... that the hideous dream didn't happen...

Ding!

(ANGELICA) Running 1hr behind.

So sorry.

Had breakfast sent up 4 u while u wait

(Emojis heart:angel halo:heart)

(ME) All good

Thks for letting me know

The very thought of eating makes me want to hurl, however, the Princess Bride behind schedule is one thing I'll take as a win.

He's waiting when I emerge from the bathroom.

He smiles with his liquid eyes and perfect teeth, but no Matey! That's not getting you anywhere with me.

He hesitates for a second, then blurts out -

"You know... I really like your sister."

I'm blindsided. I don't know what I'm supposed to say to that because *what the actual fuck*, right...?

And what the hell is going on...?

My sister is having some kind of relationship with the other half of the Wedding of the Year?

Oh, and apparently he *does* know I'm her sister...

"It's just the timing. It's ..."

He falters. I help him out.

"Completely fucked...?"

He laughs ruefully.

"I was going to go with *all wrong*, but completely fucked better captures the essence of it."

Hmmm...

Awkward...

All I can do Is shake my head and avoid eye contact as I make a very welcome escape.

Could this Birthday possibly get any weirder...?

No.

It could not.

Could it...?

I knock softly on the door of the presidential suite of the beyond five star Palace Hotel. It's swiftly opened by Danh Le - hair and make-up magician to the stars.

One look at me and the serene smile disappears from his face.

"Food poisoning. I was up *all night...*"

Lovely Larry isn't the only liar in the family.

He helps me drag the baggage cart carrying all my stuff into the room.

"There's a bar just through here to the left. It'll make a good work space for you. There's running water. And marble floor, so it's okay if you make a mess... And there's food on the dining table if you're up to eating."

Danh's a thinker - and a consummate professional. He's already set up - make up chair in the morning sunlight... palettes, bottles, brushes, sponges lined up with surgical precision.

There's a rack of wedding dresses, a mountain of shoe boxes and a coffee table covered with rows of jewellery and tiaras. It's looking suspiciously like she still doesn't have a plan. Which is why I'm here. Usually any flowers for the bride's hair would be done the day before, but given our Insta-Princess didn't have to make decisions months in advance (like everyone else), I'm having to make Insta-Flower Magic. Now, to anyone else this is when Troy would say *Sorry - we're not the florist for you...* but when you're a Mancini and you spend the equivalent of the GDP of a small country with Le Jardin every year...

So I prepped everything I thought I could possibly need yesterday and I'm praying this will be quick and painless.

Soon as I'm unpacked and set up, Danh points at me, then points to his chair.

You. Sit.

"No!" I'm horrified. "We can't do that! That is so unprofessional. Where is she...?"

"She just went down to the gym with her personal trainer, so we've got at least an hour. I only need twenty-five minutes... And it's hurting me to look at you."

I hesitate, then tell myself if I look better I might feel better. And I really do need to feel better. It's going to be a very long day. Fleetingly I wonder if a shower is an option, because that would be *really* good right now...

Danh throws deodorant and curiously Bettadine sore throat gargle at me.

"Your breath. Trust me."

"Can I grab some toast and coffee first...? Because I feel like..." My voice trails off. There is no adequate word to describe my current physical and mental state.

"Oh Babe... You *look* like..."

I kinda know Danh - he sometimes works with Simon and I often bump into him when I get to be the Plus One at industry schmoozes.

"Your skin's pretty good... what do you use...?"

"Oh... I dunno... whatever Simon leaves in the bathroom..."

He's always coming home from jobs with free stuff and it'd be rude not to test it, wouldn't it...? And is it just me, or did Danh do a little rapid intake of breath when I mentioned Simon...?

"So... is Simon doing that Seven video...?"

He asks casually. Actually, I think he's trying a little too hard to sound casual. I wave Yes, trying not to choke on Bettadine.

"Oh..." He sounds more than a little disappointed. "They wanted me, but they couldn't promise it'd wrap last night and I had to be here..."

No.

It's not just me.

That's more than Casual Interest. Make mental note to tell Simon.

I pour myself some coffee - which smells like heaven and hope - then I slather a piece of rye toast in butter before strategically dotting it with Vegemite. (It's an Australian thing. I'm sorry but you'll have to get used to it.) If you love and understand Vegemite, you'll know that sometimes it's possibly the only thing that can make you feel better.

Danh is tall, cool and Vietnamese.

Glossy black hair falls stylishly over his smooth face.

Black jeans. Black t-shirt half tucked at the front to show off a Gucci belt. He found his calling when, at a very young age, he realised he was better at hair and make up than all his six older sisters put together.

He's famous for working in silence and I gotta say it's very soothing having his gentle but authoritative hands gliding over my face.

Occasionally he mutters softly *Look up... look down... look over my left shoulder... suck your cheeks in like a fish...*

Finally he stops and steps back, tilting his head critically.

Then nods and sighs with relief.

"So much better..."

I go to get up but he stops me.

"Hang on. We've got time for hair. I'm thinking a braid to the side - but will that drive you nuts while you're working?"

I shrug.

Whatever.

Right now my priority is staying upright for the next hour. Baby steps.

I try not to splutter as he blasts my head with dry shampoo, then fall into a little trance as he brushes, parts, gently pulls and twists my hair.

"Ever thought about colouring your hair...? You'd make a great redhead..." Danh muses thoughtfully.

"Been there. Done that. It required commitment..."

A quick flashback to a hairdresser's chair in Soho... wincing in the mirror as a cheeky little cocktail hat was forcibly secured to my head for the races at Ascot... a gleaming, sleek chin-length bob 'the colour of an autumn leaf' - like F. Scott Fitzgerald's Jordan Baker. It met the same fate as everything else in my life at the time that also expected me to commit...

He stands back and gives a little nod of affirmation.

Then he holds up a mirror.

"Oh... Fa-ark!!!"

I do recognise myself, but it's an airbrushed, healthy, well-rested and photo-shopped smooth'n'glowy version. My eyes look bigger, my nose looks smaller, my skin looks perfect. I somehow have cheekbones.

"Thank you so much! You are..."

I can't find the word to describe his awesomeness.

"I know right..." he says with a shrug.

I'm checking in with work, letting them know I haven't even started yet, when the suite door bursts open.

There's our lovely bride - all damp and glowing with excitement and endorphins - followed by her pretty young PA who's juggling a bunch of tech equipment and a Pomeranian who's had his fur trimmed to look like a teddy bear. All of them - Pomeranian included - are wearing activewear emblazoned with a stylised halo, the logo for Angelica's *Angel* lifestyle brand.

"Good morning!" she beams, then her pretty brow furrows. "I'm so sorry to hold you up, Cressida. We *crushed* Insta this morning..."

"So... about The Plan..." Danh begins hesitantly. He glances nervously at the rack of frocks, then stares pointedly at his watch.

"Oh I know!" she wails. "It's just... I've narrowed it down to two... and they're both by designers I'm really close to... so whoever's dress I *don't* pick..."

She looks at us imploringly, then pulls them off the rack. Diplomacy is a problem when you're a Princess...

"And they're completely different. *This* is what everyone will be expecting..."

Strapless, barely hoo-hoo length, covered in sequins.

"But I'm in love with this one too! It's not me at all - but I kinda like that it's so unlikely. And it would make my parents so happy..."

The Disney Princess dress. Boned bodice. A million layers of soft, floaty tulle.

Everyone stands staring at the dresses for an inordinate amount of time, waiting for Anjelica to figure it out.

"Wear both of them."

The words just came out of my mouth - and it's probably not my place - but if I don't start doing something soon, I'm going to need to have a lie down.

Slowly, every head - including the Pomeranian - turns to look at me.

"Wear the romantic dress to the church, then change into the sexy dress for the reception."

"Oh! You're a genius!"

No. I'm just a girl who's really tired...

Dilemma solved, Anjelica springs into action, culling the mountain of accessories into a short list for each dress.

"How do we feel about this tiara for the Princess dress...? I like it, but it's a bit..."

"Austere."

And those words just keep falling out of my mouth, don't they?

"Yes! Austere."

"Hang on - "

I disappear to the bar, then return with a handful of tiny, wired flowers and foliage - palest pink baby rosebuds... delicate white stephanotis... tiny, glossy green leaves... I place a few in between the blindingly sparkly stones.

"I can customise the tiara with flowers... See how they soften it...? And it'll be a more unique look."

Everyone nods. Customised, soft, unique look - those words hit all the right spots.

"Oh I love it!"

Happy bride, happy florist. Happy central nervous system. I pick up some pretty little diamanté hair pins.

"I could do something similar on these for the other dress to tie the two looks together."

Happy bride is now so delighted she hugs me.

"So... hair up then hair down...?" asks Danh.

"How about something like Cressida's done with her hair for the reception...?"

We glance at each other slyly and try not to laugh.

"I think I can manage that..." Danh smirks.

She holds a jewelled cuff up against her perfect, tiny, bronzed bicep.

"This is supposed to go with the sequin dress but... does it say *Bride*...? I'm concerned I'm going to look like I'm going to any old party."

"Hang on..."

Again I disappear to the bar, returning with some wire and some more flowers.

"How about a cuff made of flowers...?"

Quickly I twist a few things together and hold it against her upper arm.

"Perfect!"

She places a peach manicured hand over mine and squeezes, looking me in the eye with the tiniest tears welling.

"Thank you so much!"

My mind goes to her rat fiancé and my rat sister... I give my head a little shake to make it go away.

Quickly I change the subject.

"Can I just grab a measurement for your arm...?"

The toast and coffee has settled my stomach and chirped me up a little. And having to focus on the painstaking job of wiring teeny flowers takes my mind off my questionable physical state, and stops it replaying the memory of the girl getting thrown in the van and the dog getting thrown in the dumpster. I'm in the zone, in my work bubble.

And quickly I get the job done, including a cute little garland for the little dog to wear.

"So... Everybody happy...?"

Yes. Everyone - including the Pomeranian - is delighted. He smiles obligingly for the camera as I take a quick snap of him for Le Jardin's socials.

"I'll be downstairs in the ballroom all afternoon, so if you need anything tweaked just text me."

Carefully I clean up my mess.

Every leaf, every petal, every tiny bit of stem and wire. We're spoilt in the workroom where everything falls on the floor and junior minions sweep it up.

Ding!

Simon. Again. Bless.

Better yet...?

I shoot back the eyes-but-no-mouth Emoji.

(ME) Better is big word

Currently happy with Upright

As I look up from my phone, Angelica is right next to me. She gives me a goodbye hug.

"Thank you so much, Cressida! I love working with you."

Naw... ! I hug her toned, tiny body back.

"Good luck!" - and I mean it in more ways than our poor bride can know...

I'd called to let them know I'm heading back, making a quick detour via the Mc DriveThru for a hash brown and a McMuffin. I think treating whatever the hell is wrong with me like a hangover (ie. steadily drip-feeding fat and salt) could be a winner.

As I slide the heavy back door to the bunker open, the entire workroom bursts into a fast-forward version of ...

HappyBirthdaytoyouHappyBirthdaytoyou

HappyBirthdaydearKitty-Ka-aa-at...

HappyBirthdaytoyou!

...as Troy produces a super-elaborate chocolate mousse cake, covered with ganache and architectural chocolate swirly things.

"Grab cake. Eat fast. Back to work. No talking!"

Yes Boss!

There's a bunch of orders (oh... no pun intended...) waiting on my work station. I get stuck into it.

I've been working here a couple of years and I've quite quickly become Troy's Favourite Child because I'm creative, I'm fast, I do good work and I have a knack for understanding what the client is after. 'Bright - but not too bright' or 'feminine without being girly' or 'modern but not kooky' - I get all that.

My love of flowers started with Gran. As I never got picked for the netball team (and it's really not something I lost any sleep over...) or never had Larry's pathological need to perform, TBJ would drop me with the grandparents while she took Miranda to Saturday morning sport and Larry to lessons or rehearsals. Sometimes we'd go to their country house for the whole weekend, and in so many of my happiest memories I'm here... getting dirty in the garden... inhaling the sweet, warm smell of the stables... thundering across paddocks and sailing over fences... helping grown-ups fix all things animal, vegetable and mineral - from broken fences, to struggling rhododendron bushes, to orphaned calves and abandoned kittens.

Both in town and in the country, Gran loves her outside spaces - rambling, shady havens on the wild side of English Country Garden. When I was a little girl, it felt like a fantasy land - so vast, private and quiet. Helping Gran plant, water, prune, weed and dead-head, I came to the conclusion that every flower is an astonishing creation in its own right.

When I started working as a florist (which happened quite by accident - but that's another story for another day...) I learnt I could make them so much more, letting them tell so many stories by putting them in different contexts.

I knock out a couple of pretty Happy Birthdays, a Thank You for Dinner (small, tasteful but exquisite) and an elaborate 80's retro arrangement for a table for two that involved minions air-brushing roses various shades of pink to match the French variety, Fantin Latour. The emailed order is so specific - complete with photo references - the probability of Max Black finding something to be unhappy about is alarmingly high... which always makes us nervous...

Libby calls out my name.

Libby is in charge of Air Traffic Control here - she answers the phones, coordinates the diaries and assigns the mountain of orders to the right florist for the job.

And keeps us all in line.

As a single mum with four teenage kids whose husband left her for his PA, this is one of three jobs she works. Her posh phone voice is somewhat different to the Mum voice she often resorts to in an attempt to restore order when we get a bit raucous.

"There's an order for Larry. Do you want it?"

My breath catches in my throat and I stiffen. I try to keep my voice casual.

"Oh! Who's it from..?"

Libby raises her eyebrows theatrically and lowers her voice to a sultry and mysterious register.

"Anonymous! It appeared on the shop counter - instructions, card, cash... It was busy so no-one noticed who..."

I take a deep breath. I already know who they're from, and I already know more than I want to.

Now don't get me wrong - I like a bit of fun as much as the next girl.

But I don't like games and I don't like infidelity. Someone else's man is just that - *someone else's*. So I'm really not crazy about her doing whatever it is she's doing full stop. And I'm especially not crazy about her doing it with the fiancé of someone whose father is rumoured to reinforce foundations with dead bodies.

So I lie.

"I've still got a bit to do... I'll have to handball it to someone else if it needs to go out on the twelve pick up..."

If this was a normal Saturday, we'd be in the home straight by now. Orders just about finished, leftover flowers beginning to be spirited into the cool-rooms for when we reopen on Monday and the giant glass front door about to be locked.

However this is Monster Wedding Saturday.

The boys from Hangry - the cafe in the side street that we pretty much keep in business - arrive with trays of chicken caesar and tuna salad wraps, plus a selection of cupcakes, brownies and donuts.

"Right!" Troy is jangling a bunch of keys. "Soon as you're finished, grab some food and get in a van. *Please* have your phone on you - we can't be fucking around trying to find people all afternoon in that freaking hotel!... Kitty-Kat, you're riding with me."

Instantly I regret picking the double chocolate cupcake, seeing dark gooey crumbs all over the cream leather seats of his Mercedes convertible.

I know there's some eye-rolling going on behind my back. For most part, we're a big happy family, but I know there are a few people who feel I haven't worked my way up through the ranks to earn my stripes here, and are a bit resentful how quickly I've become Troy's Right Hand Girl.

And I guess I can't blame them. However on this occasion, they should just settle down.

Because I know Troy's only chosen me because not knowing every single thing that happened with Angelica this morning will be killing him.

Speak now...
or forever hold your peace...

The cloudless sky is a brilliant bright blue, and the sun is hot and blinding. Thankfully he puts the top up and turns on the aircon as I recount my morning in minute detail (whilst kinda perpetuating the food poisoning lie...)

We're a couple of blocks from the hotel and the one'o'clock news is on the radio.

"They'd better be ready for us ..." mutters Troy as he glances ominously at the clock. This afternoon is going to be hell.

Generally we'd be pretty much done by now for a function of this size. We would have got most of the set up done yesterday, with just a few last minute things to drop in today. However, as misfortune would have it, there was a massive industry awards ceremony in the ballroom last night. Before we can even start, everything has to be bumped out, the colossal room has to be cleaned, then the tables and chairs for tonight need to be pretty much in place. Otherwise us and the guys from Epic Events are going to be falling all over each other (and ordinarily, one wouldn't mind falling over those Epic boys, because they're generally a bit hot... but sadly there won't be time for flirtation today...) Everyone's promised us they'll be good to go by one.

The chirpy newsreader tells us it's a ridiculous thirty-two degrees, and then...

Police are appealing to the general public for information relating to an incident that occurred last night between the hours of midnight and one pm in the Carlton/ North Melbourne area. If you witnessed any suspicious activity, please call the hotline on...

I snap to attention and stare wide-eyed at the radio. My pulse starts thudding in my ears..

I. Saw. It. All.

But how do I know it's real?

No.

It was just a dream.

Don't be ridiculous.

But what if it isn't just a dream???

They have to find her. He is a monster.

I don't want to find out what he does next. I feel sick at the mere thought of having to watch it.

"Kitty-Kat... Kitty-Kat! Earth to Miss Kitty! Let's go!"

I haven't even noticed that Troy has parked the car and he's half out the door waiting impatiently for me.

I'm still staring at the radio.

We make our way through the maze of service corridors that run around the ballroom. And my head keeps going round the same loop -

the red sneakers... Bear's body... her face... his voice...

" *...if you witnessed suspicious activity...*"

I tell Troy I have to go to the loo, then find a quiet corner in the chaos. I pull out my phone, almost hoping there's no reception so I'm off the hook.

Damn! Three bars.

With an unsteady hand I punch in the number.

A bored, monotone female voice tells me I have called the Police Hotline. My thumb hovers over the red button.

This is a bad idea. Hang up.

The red sneakers, Bear's body, her face, his voice...

I take a deep breath, then trying to modulate my voice so I'm less likely to sound like a nutcase -

"I saw three men in a white van abduct a girl last night."

There's a pause, then she starts speaking in a voice that's a lot more interested. She asks where and I tell her. I know the streets between Melbourne Uni and Dad's Queen Street chambers like the back of my hand.

"Where were you and what time was this?'

I take a very deep breath.

This is when it's going to start getting awkward.

"I was at home. I'm unsure of the exact time."

"And where is that?"

I inhale very slowly through my nose.

Just say it.

"South Yarra."

"Could you repeat that, please?"

There's no turning back now. I repeat the suburb, and elaborate with the exact address.

"I'm unsure of the exact time because I was asleep. I saw it in a dream."

There is a *very* long pause.

"Right."

She sounds pissed off and her voice is patronising.

"Miss Carlisle, if you really feel the need to make a statement, you can come in one day next week.'

She doesn't believe me.

Which isn't unreasonable, because I'm not even sure that I believe me. But then I remember Bear.

In the dumpster.

And I blurt out -

"But what about the dog!!!"

She is silent for a few beats, then asks cautiously -

"What about the dog? What dog?"

"Bear. Her Golden Retriever. They hurt him and threw him in a dumpster, but I don't think he's dead... but he won't last long in this heat...!"

Suddenly she wants me to go in for an interview today.

Sorry - can't! - working.

I give her the precise location of the laneway and the dumpster.

She confirms my address and phone number, instructs that someone will come to interview me first thing tomorrow morning, then hangs up.

I stand there, staring at my phone with my head swimming.

She knows about Bear.

Bear is real.

The girl is real.

What I saw is...*real*...?

And I don't know if that makes it better or worse... because hey! At least I'm not going crazy. However I'm not sure that having horrific visions while you're sleeping is an entirely sane thing to do.

And then the most hideous realisation of all...

If this is real... the cell is real... the chain is real.

He is real.

My stomach convulses, my lunch is back in my mouth and I really am needing to find the nearest loo.

I stand in the service corridor outside the ballroom and take a long, slow breath before launching myself into it... hoping my breath doesn't smell of bile and regurgitated lunch.

The epic 'room' - the size of a football field - looks like the scene of a military campaign. An army (of hot guys in Epic Events t-shirts) has swept from the front to the back, setting up one hundred tables and one thousand delicate, gilded chairs around the great sea of a dance floor with centimetre perfect precision. The dark dance floor gleams like a lake - inky, midnight blue glass. Photocopied signs are placed around it at three foot intervals - *KEEP THE FUCK OFF!!!!!* Someone will trail dirty footprints across it. Somebody always does.

Troy is at the long, bare bridal table, scanning the room impatiently. Looking for me.

He's reaching for his phone as I appear at his side.

"Sorry. I had to hurl."

"Too much information. Now... get on this with me. The clock's ticking..."

Central Park at Midnight is the theme.

Which is where and when he asked her to marry him... which seems achingly romantic... until one juxtaposes it with one's sister's g-string flying through the air - ironically the same shade of pink as the bride's Royal Highness roses...

Just as well the budget is *spare no expense* because to turn this incomprehensibly gigantic space into anything requires expense.

Incomprehensibly Gigantic Expense. Real trees were not an option. Apart from being logistically impossible, tree trunks are a visual nightmare that block everyone's view of everything. So... we had specially designed vases custom-made.

Shaped like an hourglass - so there's enough weight at the bottom to counter-balance the top - each one is five feet tall and sits in the middle of every table. The arrangement at the top consists of lush tree branches that were 'pruned' yesterday from Troy's country garden (and anybody else's garden from whom we could call in a favour...) The leaves have very fortunately not thought about changing colour yet, given April in New York is... well... Spring, not Autumn.

Each branch is dusted with fairy lights, then softened with some very real-looking baby pink artificial blossom and strategically-placed dainty little pale pink, amethyst and Tiffany-blue glass lanterns, each holding a tiny candle.

When we're done, the whole room will be under a canopy of foliage, blossom and twinkling lights. A midnight blue sky with a million sparking stars will be projected onto the ceiling and the walls.

Each vase sits on a large, circular mirror to reflect the lights and the leaves. (And has the added advantage that we can top up the vases without being super-paranoid about spilling water on the immaculate leaf-green damask table cloths.) Also sitting on the mirror is a wild garland of foliage and baby pink roses, strategically dotted with tea lights.

It will look like a magical fairytale - if it ever gets finished.

Running the length of the bridal table is a matching garland. We did the garlands yesterday, so putting them all in place is the easy part. Framing the bridal table like a proscenium arch is a spectacular arbour.

Which we need to build.

Which begins with the Epic boys constructing a giant frame.

Right on cue, Rory appears.

Tall, dark and Irish. And naughty.

They do a lot of heavy lifting and carrying, so they're all in good shape. In Rory's case, the *Epic* written across his exemplary pectorals is somewhat superfluous.

And right on cue, sound check of the state of the art system starts... Wailing guitars... bluesy, sultry bass... and drums better suited to strip club than a fairytale wedding. I think it's a pretty safe bet that Led Zeppelin is not on tonight's playlist. I go to speak, but he holds up a finger, pausing for a second before lip-synching perfectly with the super sexy vocal.

I'm obligated to roll my eyes and shake my head at him because, well, no! We do not have time for flirting today... however... given I haven't had any in nearly a year, shaking him all night long isn't sounding like a bad idea...

"So... Pretty Kitty..."

Ah yes. And then there's the irresistible Irish accent. And the cheeky, twinkling eyes.

"You're needing me for an erection..."

"Yep. And I quite urgently need you to get it up *really, really* fast..."

"Oh for you I can get it up fast..."

"You say that to all the girls..."

I help him start organising the poles and clamps for our 'erection'.

Soon as we have our frame, Troy and I start in the centre - right behind where our 'happy' couple will be seated - and work our way outwards. We're both four feet up ladders with a Junior

Minion at the bottom, handing up each thing we need as it's required.

Crepe Suzette is assisting me. Just out of school with possessed blond pre-Raphaelite curls down to her waist and clear, pale blue eyes. There's an other worldly innocence about her.

She's still blushing from Rory saying *erection.*

Another six months with us and she'll be constructing entire sentences using only obscenities...

Suzette is actually her real name.

Troy naturally added the Crepe as an aide-memoir..

Ding!

Yep. Simon. Again. Bless!

Doin' ok...???

Worried about you

Quickly I send him a *heart,* then shove my phone into a pocket of my cargoes... before Troy growls at me.

"What does that bit at the back look like...?"

Suzette's trying to hold up branches of oak nearly as big as her tiny frame so I can find the perfect shaped one to fill a gap.

"Hmmm... no... maybe the first one..."

"You always pick the first one..." she says with a quiet smile.

"Well, yes..." I concede. "But it's always good to check out your options..."

"Same goes for men, girls..."

Troy winks at us, deftly stripping some foliage from a branch with one hand. Poor Crepe Suzette doesn't know where to look.

Foliage.

Lights.

Lanterns.

We work steadily, carefully and efficiently, eventually arriving at the furthermost ends at almost the same time. The rest of the crew has set up a production line to work through the monster table centres. They're about a third of the way through the room.

Without saying a word, we join them.

To say this is less than ideal is beyond understatement.

We could not be any further from fucking ideal.

Each one is so huge and heavy they have to be done on the ground next to their intended table, then carefully... agonisingly... lifted up. Potential for making mess - and a litany of other disasters - is alarmingly high.

I instruct Crepe Suzette to grab an empty monster vase, I grab an armful of oak branches that are overwhelmingly bigger than me, and we wrestle our way to the next-in-line table.

While I artfully - but quickly as possible - create my 'tree', I send Suzette back to the service corridor for a watering can and our lanterns.

I can hear Troy calling out directions as he gets stuck into a vase. He is in his element. Like a conductor directing Shostako-vich... treading the fine line between chaos and genius... and despite the potential for everything to fall apart in the second movement, it's looking like yet again he's going to pull it off.

"Ginger! That branch at the back is too low! Anyone over six foot is going to knock the whole thing over - which would be the Mother of all fucking disasters... Mavis, that's looking a bit mean on the lanterns - are there fifteen...? Each one must have fifteen, yes...?"

And then he bursts into a medley of tunes from Chigao to amuse himself and anyone else within earshot.

"Thanks Crepe!" I say as she helps me finish adding the lanterns, then holds some foliage up out of the way as I wiggle the spout of a watering can into the vase to half-fill it.

"Right!"

I take a deep breath, glance at the table to mentally calculate how far up and over I need to lift this fucker, then give it the Eye of the Tiger as I mentally prepare myself to do it.

So near, and yet so far.

I bend my knees, ducking my head and shoulders under the canopy of leaves. I hug my arms around the glass, bracing myself to pick it up when -

"*Jesus Cressida!* You shouldn't be lifting that! Here - let me –"

Oh Rory! (...and can anyone say *Jey-sus* quite like an Irishman...? No. They cannot.)

"Rory, I lift vases that weigh more than I do all day. Really - it's fine. I'll be a bit sore tomorrow... and I possibly won't be able to have children..."

"We can't have that! You'd look beautiful with a big belly..."

"Behave!... and not happening..."

He carefully lifts it up over the table, then carefully places it on the mirror. I help him wiggle it into place.

90

Those tree branches will suck through a gallon of water. I instruct Suzette to top up the vase right to the brim.

"Hey - my lads are just about done... can we help you ladies - " he grins cheekily, including the boys Ginger, Mavis and Earl (also not their real names)... " - with some heavy lifting...? Or anything really..."

"Oh I've got something heavy you can lift..." Earl is looking at Rory's pecs like they're dessert.

"Don't say it if you don't mean it, Big Boy!" Rory counters with a sassy wink.

"Oh! *Behave!* Yes! We'll take whatever help we can get... If your guys can place the vases, then fill them like Crepe Suzette is doing now - that would be swell!"

Every time-consuming thing we don't have to do helps bring the finishing line closer into view.

And quite quickly half of the floor turns into three quarters complete. The Epic army of waiting staff has arrived to set the tables. Each piece of stemware and flatware will be placed in front of every chair with millimetre perfect precision. Every glass polished crystal clear. Every fork, knife and spoon gleaming like a mirror.

Come 5.30pm, we're done. Right on time to begin the lighting of the five hundred million candles and tea lights. When your Dad basically owns the hotel and you *really* dislike LED candles, any complications of naked flames and insurance policies don't apply to you. We begin at the periphery and work our way inwards to the bridal table, so the focal point tables will still be burning at the end of the party. Everyone is handed a gas gun or lighter and starts click-click-clicking.

At 6.25pm - five minutes before the elevator doors will open to reveal Fairyland to Ash and Angelica's guests - I light the last candle on the arbour. We all quickly cast hawk eyes over the room, checking that every ladder, watering can and any other menial thing that reduces the illusion to reality has been removed.

As we turn to leave, sighing with relief and finally beginning to smile with self-congratulations, an amethyst lantern slips from its perch and plummets groundwards. Rory dives at it like a cricket ball that's been hit for Four!... and disaster is averted.

I look in vain for a ladder to put it back, but of course there isn't one. And there's no time to find one.

Then Rory's hands are around my waist.

"On three, jump!"

"I'm too heavy! Don't be ridiculous -"

"I can deadlift one-eighty. A little Kitty won't be a problem. Now come on woman! We don't have time to have a fight about it."

I have no idea what lifting one-eighty means, but I'm guessing it's more than me. So on three, I channel my inner-kitty and jump lithely up to the arbour, secure the lantern, then extract a lighter from the pocket on my thigh.

And with one final Click!... the Wedding of the Year is (once again!) good to go.

Ping!

Distant elevator doors open to a babble that sounds like a remote flock of flamingoes. The guests will walk in at precisely the same moment that we step out..

Swoosh!

Rory and I release the catches on the pair of swinging double doors to the service corridor. Which is now empty. A service elevator rattles back up from depositing everyone else in the basement carpark and the doors slide open. We step in and reach for the button at the same time, laughing a little awkwardly as our hands crash together.

Rory yawns and stretches. His t-shirt rides up, revealing a glimpse of six-pack and a belly button.

Earth to Cressida!

And you're busted. He catches me staring.

"You know, I always thought Kitty-Kat was just another of Troy's silly names... I can't believe I've never noticed your eyes before... they really are just like a cat!"

Hmmmm... you haven't noticed them because I generally don't have someone spending forty minutes making them look fetching... However, this kind of attention makes me kinda awkward.

Oh God!

Say something.

Anything.

"Thanks for helping us out today. I owe you one. Big time." I blurt it out, possibly a little too fast.

Ding!

Oh thank God! An excuse to look away as I fish my phone out of my pocket.

You know who it is...

Need a ride babe???

Quickly I send back

All good. Will get lift with Troy

Home soon

Unfortunately when I look up from my phone, Rory is still considering me in an uncomfortably thoughtful manner.

"You could come out for a drink with me. To say Thank You..."

Ding!

Saved by the bell.

The lift doors open on our respective armies packing their convoys of vans after another successful campaign.

We both step out. I stare up at him with a slightly perplexed frown. Because in the nearly two years I've been at Le Jardin, Rory has jokingly propositioned me on a weekly basis. Never missing the opportunity for a double entendre or a highly suggestive suggestion. And I'm very comfortable with that. I can give it right back. Earnest Rory I am not comfortable with...

There are no Rules of Engagement.

"I mean it."

Hmmm... that's what worries me...

He's looking down at me, smiling.

"You should have a drink with me sometime."

Still frowning, wondering if this added weirdness is something else caused by the trajectory of Saturn through the sky after midnight, I kinda smile back at him. For once, I got nothin' smart-ass or sassy to throw back. And seriously, I haven't kissed a boy in so long I'm wondering if I remember how...

"Hmmm... maybe...? You know where to find me!"

It's nearly seven when Troy drops me home.

Dog-tired, but relieved the job got done - even if by the skin of our teeth. I'm very glad that's not how we usually roll, because it was not pleasant. But at least being frantically busy meant I couldn't think about any of the disturbing things swirling around my brain's periphery...

The girl... the cell... Bear's body... pale pink knickers flying through the air...

I haul my exhausted ass up the stairs.

Simon flings the door open before I can find my keys, holding out a tall glass of something pink for me.

"Oh!"

Pleasantly surprised and slightly confused by my appearance, then a much lower pitched *oh!* as he remembers I worked with Danh today. He gives my face a critical appraisal.

"God he's good!"

And there's something in his voice that suggests his admiration may be more than just professional...

"Happy Birthday You! Where are we going...? And don't you give me any of that whiny *I'm tired* nonsense, Missy! You have to go out looking like that!"

I hold up a finger to stop him, take the glass out of his hand, take a big slurp, then hand it back.

"Shower! Or I'm going to die."

"But we are going out, right...? And don't mess up your makeup! You look hot!"

Peeling the clothes from my sweaty body, I don't think I've ever been so glad to see my bathroom. Turning a room that is essentially the size of a football field into an awe-inspiring Wonderland in record time was hot, hard work. I take a deep breath and with trepidation, prepare to remove yesterday's (now filthy) Bandaids from my finger.

No festering mess! Yay. Winning.

I spin the cold tap to full blast, then add the tiniest dash of hot.

Simon replaced the shower head with something that's basically bigger than my head, removing all those 'pesky' water-saving filters. So at least our dated and inadequate bathroom has the mother of all power showers.

Mmmmm!

The lukewarm water feels so good cascading over my body - though it'd be a whole lot more satisfying if I could stick my head and face in there too... however I must say my face has been a very pleasant surprise every time I've passed a reflective surface today...

I emerge from my bedroom feeling pretty good in a black camisole, a short, flippy paisley skirt and some groovy retro cork platform sandals. Most of my wardrobe - and a lot of our furniture - is stuff Simon gets to bring home from photo shoots. Often it's just given away - the client who paid for it has no use for it. Other times - as in the case of our super sexy ink blue velvet four-seater

98

sofa - a ridiculously nominal hundred or so will get the goodies home.

Simon looks up from some rapid-fire left/right swiping, gives me a critical once over, then an approving nod.

I sink into said sexy sofa, as Simon hands me back my pomegranate and vodka cocktail (which is absolute heaven after the hot'n'hectic job from hell...) and starts to ask me about my day, then he interrupts himself, as he often does...

"Hang on! Last night!!! What the fuck happened to you? OMG! I thought you were dead! I couldn't wake you up!"

So I tell him everything.

The dream... Larry and Ash Knight... The Bride... Larry's Anonymous flowers...

"Hang on... Stop! We need a refill..."

The Police Hotline... The Reception Room... Epic Rory maybe actually liking me...?

He stares at me in wide-eyed astonishment.

"Fa-aa-aa-aa-aark! That is mental!"

"I know, right. Every time I thought this day cannot possibly get any weirder..."

My voice trails off....

"So you did a Grandma Delia...??? You really think you had a Psychic Moment???"

"At dinner last night she did say something big was going to happen after midnight..."

"And you think it *did*???" he asks with the beautiful, wide-eyed incredulity of a toddler.

"I dunno... You know I always have crazy dreams, but this was different. Every single detail was crystal clear... like I was actually living it... And I *feel* like I lived it... I think there might be something in it... soon as I mentioned the dog, her attitude changed completely."

I remember the sickening noise as Bear's ribs collapsed and I shudder. I take another big gulp.

The bittersweet pink stuff is numbing me nicely.

Every glass distances me a little bit further from the mess in my head.

"God I hope they found him in time and he's okay..."

"And the girl..." Simon frowns.

"Maybe they've found her already...?" I try to sound hopeful, but I can't make my heart believe it. And then I remember the most important thing of all...

"Hey... Danh asked about you... He seemed really disappointed he couldn't work with you yesterday..."

Very slowly and quietly I say the magic words...

"I think he likes you."

To my surprise, Simon has a mini freak out.

He looks away.

Then he looks down.

Then when he realises he cannot look away forever, he turns back to me. And he's blushing.

"OMG! You like him too!'

He presses his lips together and nods, bright cornflower-blue eyes looking almost pained. Hmmm... they would make the cutest couple... I wonder what I can do to help things along...

"Stop it! Don't you dare do anything! Here... "

He disappears to the small third bedroom, which is his office and returns with a beautifully gift-wrapped package. Which he throws at my head.

"Happy Birthday! Have a present!"

Ripping it open reveals a black cashmere turtleneck and a grey cashmere hoodie. Soft.... Mmmmm... So soft! I give him a squeezy hug and a smoochie kiss.

"Oh! They're *insane*!!! Thank you!... "

"You're welcome - and they're *handwash only!* You're going to respect the cashmere, aren't you...? Nod three times to demonstrate you understand."

I give three little half-hearted nods, because we both know I'll be throwing them in the washing machine. Simon sighs in frustration.

"You really are that kid who can't have nice things, aren't you...?"

"Rude!" I shriek back indignantly, then divert the dialogue to a much more interesting subject... "Hey, how did your job go...? Is Tomcat Hardy really the sexiest man on the planet...?"

"Oh it was great - it's going to be really cool. And Tom is lovely. He's actually really shy and somehow has no idea how ridiculously hot he is..."

I reply with a thoughtful Hmmpf! - because that's really all you can say about that...

"So Birthday Girl..." Simon says emphatically. Apparently it's time to focus. "What do you want to do...? There's a warehouse party later, but we can do anything you like now."

"Anything...?" I say, raising a sly eyebrow.

"Oh God no... Really...? Can't we go somewhere lush for dinner or cocktails...?"

"Nope. You said anything..."

Simon sighs in resignation.

"Ugh. Let's go smack some balls around then."

Not Just a Pretty Face...

The giant fly swats surrounding the Melbourne Cricket Ground (aka the MCG... often further abbreviated to The G... because Australians don't love anything like they love a good abbreviation...) are lit up like Christmas trees. In April, this means one thing.

Football.

Australian Rules Football.

If we were a little earlier or a little later tonight, you wouldn't be driving anywhere near it, as the cars of fifty thousand fans fight to get in... then out... of the acres of grassy carparks that surround it. However with the game safely underway, our Uber can take us in the almost directly straight line north to the inner-city suburb of Fitzroy.

Football is the all-inclusive, multi-denominational religion of Melbourne. Pretty much everyone over the age of three loves their footy, and will discuss it passionately with pretty much anybody who'll listen. Truck drivers... bankers... nuns... (not to mention florists, fashion stylists and Queen Street barristers.) Dad and Grandpa predictably support Melbourne, the old school, old money team. Simon, being a Perth boy is West Coast Eagles. And I was lost from the Melbourne Demons at a young age - to Dad's distress, to this day- to Richmond, basically because I liked their tiger mascot.

Even if you have no understanding of the rules - and you'd easily be forgiven for assuming there are none... it's a hard, fast, full-contact game - it's *very* interesting viewing. Thirty-six tall, very fit guys in short shorts and sleeveless jerseys... getting very hot and sweaty... Get the picture...?

Our Uber drops us in a narrow, one-way street in Fitzroy. The inner-city suburb used to be industrial. Then it was ethnic-minorities, students and artists, now it's almost moved beyond hip and into sanitised fashionable.

It's the same story in every town, right...?

We enter what once was a factory and head up some flights of wooden stairs - which aren't much fun in platforms. The inside has been carved up into smaller spaces - offices, studios, residences. You can tell the residences - they have hostile signs about people making noise on the stairs stuck on their doors.

Finally we get to the top floor and I open the door to the Corner Pocket. It's dim, hushed and calm. The main illumination comes from the shaded lights over the pool tables. The familiar clink of balls, hushed voices and vintage Rolling Stones on very low volume is just what I need.

It's a huge, cavernous space with a soaring, open ceiling.

Dozens of tables - some full size, some pub size - with rows of old theatre seats arranged around them. There's highly questionable ancient carpet on the floor.

Luckily no-one is waiting for a table in the small cafe area, but the room looks pretty busy.

"Hey Stranger!"

A young Greek guy with glasses, his face lights up when he sees me. Costa. The building has been in his family for generations. At some stage, someone turned the top floor into a pool hall (and I still want to know how they got the tables up here...) It's now worth a gazillion dollars, but Costa won't sell out. He's holding one of the last few bastions of gritty as the suburb gets gentrified around him.

I used to live in a falling down Victorian terrace house a few blocks over when I was at uni. The infamous student share house. I spent a lot of time here because a) the beer is cheap, b) playing pool is - let's face it - very sexy when you're single and mingling, and - don't laugh! - c) I'm actually really good at it. Dad and

Grandpa take their billiards very seriously. We grew up with a full size table in the house and it was one of the ways us girls bonded with Dad.

"Ya Sou!" I say *Hi* in Greek - because I'm cool like that, lol - then ask expectantly. "How long?"

Costa shakes his head and looks mournful like only a Greek man can.

"Oh Man... It's not good. An hour at least. Most people only just got started..."

Boo! Simon and I both sigh. He's not crazy about pool, but he hates waiting even more. And he never accepts *No* that easily.

"So there's nothing you can do...? C'mon Costa - it's her Birthday and she just wants to play some pool."

"Your Birthday... ? Oh man.... There's one thing I can try, but no promises. Okay?"

He leaves the counter and leads us over to a table.

A guy has his back to us, racking up a frame. A neat navy t-shirt hangs from very nice shoulders, and new-looking jeans hug a very nice bum. It is not unlikely that both items of clothing have been ironed - which for in here is most unusual. Average height, in better than average shape.

Stocky build. Dark sandy curls cut in a short haircut that's at the fashionable end of Conservative.

"Hey Mick! How about doubles...? This is Sid and it's her Birthday."

"Costa please don't !... It's fine... really... we can wait." I plead, suddenly a bit embarrassed. Birthday or not, I'm not good at being pushy.

"Shut! Up!" Simon hisses at me. Yup. He's clocked the shoulders and bum too.

Mick turns around slowly and he looks pissed off. A little older than me, his face is tanned and outdoorsy. His expression is hard. I guess he's attractive in an Action Hero kind of way, but he's not my type. Not remotely.

However, he has a pool table and I don't... So I smile hopefully.

He looks me up and down slowly, then exhales so violently he snorts like a horse.

"Costa. I'm having a *Really Bad Day...*"

Oh, you and me both, Dude...!

"Please...? If I make the table free and the drinks on me...?" Costa plea bargains.

The promise of free stuff seems to swing it.

"Can she actually play or is she just decorative?"

Costa laughs out loud.

"I'll let you find that out for yourself, Mate."

Action Man shakes his head, sighs, then pushing his rectangular tortoiseshell glasses up his nose, hands me his cue.

"Your break, Birthday Girl. Pub Rules. Know what that is...?"

"Yup. Would you like me to clarify all of them for you or just the important ones...? Two shots on the black, no shooting backwards."

"Hmphh!..." Action Man snorts derisively. "Aren't you on the wrong side of the river, Rich Girl...?"

"Rude! And presumptive."

"Oh really...? Where'd you go to school...?"

"I'm not answering that!" I laugh dismissively. And a smidge haughty.

"Clendon, right...?" Interesting that he should choose Melbourne's poshest private girls school. And he is, unfortunately, correct.

I suddenly feel the need to clear my throat.

"And what does your Dad do...?"

"He's a barrister," I reply... maybe a little quietly.

"And I'm guessing you did Law at Melbourne, didn't you...?" Action Man is starting to look a bit smug.

I wrinkle my nose.

"Tick! Tick! Tick! Rich Girl!" he crows triumphantly.

"Hey! You two gonna be *malakes* or you gonna play pool...? You're all gonna love each other, trust me..." Costa gets his Big Greek Boss voice on. I really want to point out that I'm not the one being a wanker here, but instead mutter *malaka* under my breath so only Action Man can hear it as I take the cue out of his hand.

Costa makes the rest of the introductions. Mick is playing with a tallish Asian dude with floppy boyband hair and a body that looks like it could hold its own in a kung fu movie. His name's Andy.

I weigh the cue in my hand, feel its balance and check that it's straight. Hmmm... nice! Sleek smooth rosewood with ebony inlay. *Not* a crappy pool hall cue. Looks like *somebody* brings their own... I look over the tip, twist a bit chalk onto it and blow off the excess - I don't know if any of this is sexy. I'm not trying to be...

I roll the white ball to where I want it and bend over the table. Fleetingly I wonder if my skirt is long enough and my neckline high enough (I was only planning on playing with a gay man who feels the need to dress me like a freaking Barbie doll on a regular basis, so he's seen it all before.)

Yesterday's war wound is inconveniently exactly where I press my finger into the table to steady my hand, and it's been a while since I've played, however it's like riding the proverbial bicycle.

I hit the cue ball right in the sweet spot, sending it hurtling towards the fifteen coloured balls. With a gratifying *smack* they go spinning like a kaleidoscope all over the table.

"Whoo hoo hoo!" Andy throws his head back, chortling. "Beware Greeks bearing gifts. We have ourselves a Trojan horse!"

Thunk! Thunk! Thunk!

Three balls go down.

Simon puts his hand up.

"Actually I'm the purely decorative one..."

Costa arrives with a tray of drinks and a plate of his Grandma's spanakopita. A few years ago she tried to retire, but there was outrage. The homemade cheesey, spinachy goodness (with a hint of dill) wrapped in flaky filo pastry is an integral part of the Corner Pocket experience - and especially important when you've had more than a few beers. Or Cokes, in the case of Mick & Andy.

"Got a footy score, Mate...?" Andy asks Costa.

"Essendon three goals up at half time."

Mick's grimace would suggest that he's a supporter of the opposing team, Geelong.

We clink bottles, making 'polite and nice' as everyone says Cheers! to my Birthday. Then I turn back to the table to consider my next shot. Action Man is going down!

Mick shakes his head and laughs darkly at Costa. His face changes when he relaxes - and I have to concede that his smile is actually not unattractive. No, not my type, however undeniably... he's got a bit of that ruggedly handsome thing going on...

"We've been hustled!"

"No. Hustling is when I *pretend* I can't play... let you think its your idea to suggest we play for money... then I whoop your ass..."

I give him my cutest, most innocent smile as I sink another ball.

"Ima just gonna whoop your asses..."

"And they're both *very* nice asses..." Simon mutters under his breath.

I can't get anything else down, so I leave the white ball in a really ugly place. I go to turn away from the table, but Mick is right behind me. He reaches slowly to take the cue out of my hand.

But I don't let go.

"There are other cues..." I hang on, direct and determined.

"But this is actually *my* cue..." His reply is equally determined and uncompromising.

"But I like it..."

"So do I... because *it's mine!!!*"

"You gifted it to me!"

"I *loaned* it to you... hang on! Actually you just stole it."

"No terms or conditions were specified. It is therefore a gift."

"You're going legal on me...? Seriously...?"

"Aw c'mon... it's my Birthday!" - with a pretend pout that Lovely Larry would be proud of.

"Cute won't cut it with me, Rich Girl... looks like we're sharing."

"Did you just try to give me a nickname...?"

"No. I gave you a Mick-name."

"Dad Jokes...? *Seriously...?*" I shoot right back at him, wincing.

His face is completely deadpan, but there's the faintest twinkle in his eyes. Up close, I notice they're every colour of the ocean. The two-day growth on his chin looks kind of cool. However what kind of asshole doesn't let the Birthday Girl win...?!

Strong fingers curl around the cue, gently but uncompromisingly taking it off me. At the risk of soundly like Lovely Larry, I'm not accustomed to not getting my own way at the pool table, and Action Man here has most certainly *not* earned the right to get familiar. I was going to try to play nicely, but I am now very determined to annihilate him.

"How do you like my leave, Action Man...?" I ask sweetly, glancing back at my handiwork on the table.

Mick laughs darkly, shaking his head. Then he runs a hand through his hair and pushes his glasses up his nose as he considers his options, before sliding a confident hand along the table, lining up his shot.

"Bring it, Rich Girl!... Bring it!"

He not only extracts the white ball, but manages to get two more of his own down in a tricky cannon shot. He looks up from the table and raises an eyebrow at me.

"You were saying...?"

He leaves the white ball in an almost impossible spot for Simon.

"May I make a suggestion...?" as Simon turns to the table looking slightly bewildered, more interested in his conversation with Andy about cold drip coffee than winning the game.

Now not that Simon is a *bad* pool player, he's just not very strategic ... and very easily distracted.

"Nope. No coaching, Rich Girl."

"Rude! Well you're no fun at all..."

"Says the girl who started with the trash talk. And actually, I'm a barrel of goddam monkeys."

"Somehow I seriously doubt that, Action Man."

And this is why I like pool. I'm not great at talking to people I don't know. The first thing that comes into my head is usually smart-ass and easily misinterpreted as rude. So this exchange of one liners and talking around the game lets me interact without offending anyone. Most of the time.

I cringe at Simon's shot.

"Ugh. You give gay men who play pool a bad name."

"Honey, I can't be good at everything - that just wouldn't be fair," he laughs. "Who's up for a beer?"

He turns to head to the bar.

Mick looks up from the table, where he's shooting fish in a barrel, cleaning up the table with the leave Simon gave him.

"Thanks but not for us, Mate. We're on call. Two more Cokes would be good."

It vaguely registers somewhere in my head that I want to ask *On call for what???*, however they're on the black, and we're a bit screwed. I try something sneaky, but it backfires and leaves the white perfectly lined up for Andy.

"Arghhhh!!!"

I turn my back to the table, go to bang the cue on the ground in frustration but suddenly remember it's good cue and that's no way to treat it, so have to settle for shaking my fists at myself so angrily I can feel my butt jiggle.

"Isn't she cute when she's pissed off....?"

I turn to Simon, as my eyes narrow and my lip curls into a snarl.

"Okay. Maybe not so much..."

With a cool, confident arrow-straight shot, Andy sinks the black ball and they win. I shake hands with him.

"Thanks for the leave on the black!" he grins at me.

Then Mick and I shake.

"Ouch!" A spark of what feels like electricity jolts my hand.

Mick is frowning, so I know he felt it too.

"Must be the carpet..." he explains.

"Yes. The carpet... Hey, good game!"

I say it and I mean it. It was a great game - and he was a worthy adversary. He keeps hold of my hand and looks me intently in the eye.

"Not just a pretty face, huh?" he says, his voice a little softer.

"Oh I'm a woman of many, many talents!" I reply, possibly a little too loudly. A jug of cocktails and several beers will do that... hey! Did he suggest that I might be pretty...?

"Somehow I don't doubt that..." as he hands me the triangle. "Grudge match...? Rack'em up, Loser!"

He may not be my type, and he is obnoxiously cocky, but he *is* symmetrical and he can play pool. And this is just what I need to take my mind off...*that*...

After getting off to a rough start, this Birthday is not looking too bad at all.

We play for a couple of hours and we're well matched. Mick and I are taking no prisoners. Simon and Andy are more interested in talking about food. And our failed love lives.

"Look at her! How is she still single, you ask...? Oh actually I can tell you... she's fucking hopeless. No fucking idea. Makes terrible choices. Only interested in guys who aren't interested in her - the more commit-phobic and emotionally unavailable the better!"

"*You know I can hear you, right...?!*" I call them out, without looking up from the table.

"She's such a fraidy cat!"

"*I am not a fraidy cat!*" I hiss indignantly as I prowl around the table, looking for my next shot.

"Sounds like *him*..." Andy points directly at Mick. "Keeps choosing the vacuous Barbie, then breaks it off because he's bored."

"Mate, you know how I feel about you talking about me like I'm not in the room..." Mick mutters through clenched teeth.

"So they both have a flight response to genuine emotional investment...? Interesting..." Simon muses.

"You gotta stop with the psychobabble podcasts..." I laugh, shaking my head as I slide a hand down the green felt to line up my shot.

"Did her parents divorce badly...?" Andy frowns thoughtfully. "Those patterns are usually symptomatic of-"

"Nonono! They're ridiculously happy. As are her grandparents... I just want to see her happy! And her fellatio skills should now be remarkable. I made her show me her routine on a banana and it was like no-no-no!... You're doin' that all wrong..."

This over-sharing from Simon (and you do get used to it - I've learnt to find it charming) occurs just as I'm handing Mick the cue. He looks shell-shocked and fascinated in equal parts.

I show him the teensiest peek of my tongue.

He completely mis-hits the white ball and sends it flying straight off the table. After going off to retrieve it, he places it in my hand.

"Two shots, Rich Girl. *That* was dirty..."

"If you think that was dirty, you seriously need to get out more Action Man."

"Is it really your Birthday, or do you just say that to scam a game of pool...?"

"Nope... no... oh I mean yes! Yes, it *is* my Birthday...but actually, you know that's not such a bad idea..."

We level the score at three games all just as Andy's phone dings.

"Hey! Gotta run! The boss is nearly here..."

"She should come up for a game. I haven't seen her in ages... and I'd possibly be more competitive with her as a partner..."

"She's just pulled a double shift - she'll be shattered and I better not keep her waiting... and thank you. I'll remember that next time nobody else wants to play pool with you..."

He explains that his fiancé an intern at St Francis'. They're getting married in November.

"And shouldn't you be getting home to Candy...?" Andy raises a significant eyebrow as the corners of his mouth curl into a smirk. Candy? *Seriously?* Who the fuck chooses to call themself Candy...???

"Yep." Mick glances grimly at his watch. "I'm already too late. There'll be payback..."

Andy holds out his hand and we shake.

"Hey! Well played!... See you round!"

He gives Simon a friendly clap on the back, then he exchanges a dark look with Mick.

"See you tomorrow, Mate... if not before."

I'm vaguely wondering what it is that they're up to - no beer... meaningful glances - as Simon looks up from his phone.

"Party! Like just around the corner...!"

He's super-excited. He loves a party anytime, but I'm guessing from the look in his eyes that Danh is at this one.

"Are you in...? I think the guys from Seven are going.... And you look super-pretty..."

I shake my head.

"Sorry. I can think of nothing worse. I'm shattered. Thanks, Babe but rockstars or no rockstars, you'll have more fun without me tonight."

Simon's face falls as he sighs with disappointment.

"Don't worry about me. I'll just Uber home - but I need your keys... I forgot mine..."

"You always forget yours..."

Sleep... with a 90% Chance of Nightmare...

I feel like a newborn foal trying to get down the stairs in my platforms. With the added degree of difficulty of being somewhat drunk and trying to be silent when each footfall resonates with a deafening *thud!*

Eventually we get to street level, where Mick clicks the remote and a big white HiLux ute blinks its lights *Hello!* at us. I misjudge the step down onto the bluestone street. I vaguely hear Simon cry out as my ankle twists and I pitch forward face first toward the road. Mick grabs me - one hand on my arm, the other around my ribcage.

Saving me.

"Whoa! Are you okay...?"

His lips are almost on my ear as he pulls me up towards him. His hands feel safe and strong. He looks genuinely concerned, and he smells like leather, chocolate and sweat. He may not be my type, but his pheromones are starting to mess with my head.

"I don't wear grown up shoes very often... Thank you. I'll be fine now."

"I seriously doubt that, Rich Girl. I'll wait til your Uber gets here."

I'm about to insist that it's not necessary and that I've walked these streets hundreds of times... when I suddenly remember the girl in my dream... that she was thinking exactly the same thing... that she was safe...

He's standing so close I can feel the heat from his body. And I can't help but notice that it's considerably fitter than the male bodies I'm used to. However, I'm really not comfortable with this Damsel in Distress shit.

"I am perfectly capable of waiting alone..."

"But are you...?" he asks with the corners of his mouth beginning to turn up.

Honk! Honk! And an angry voice is yelling out of a car window.

"Hey! Are you going or what...?!"

Mick raises an officious hand.

"Nope. Not yet Mate..." as he waves the car along, ignoring the torrent of abuse. Inner city parking is an extreme sport on Saturday night...

My car pulls up to the curb and I give Simon a big hug.

"Have fun! Good luck with You Know Who!"

With a nervous grin and a sassy wink, he waves nighty-night to us as he disappears down the street. Meanwhile Mick has been taking a good look at the driver and seems satisfied that he's unlikely to be a serial killer. As I slide into the backseat he calls out...

"Hey! Rich Girl! Same time next week...?"

I look up to see him almost smiling. I have to admit that was actually fun. Why not...?

"You got yourself a date, Action Man!"

Oh shit! I need to clarify that. What if he thinks...

"Not like a *date* date... we're just going to..."

But the Uber has pulled away from the curb and he can't hear me. He's shaking his head and laughing.

I often have that effect on men...

The calm, quiet dark of the back seat and the purr of the engine is soothing after a long, long chaotic day. Like a kid falling asleep in the car on the way home from the grown ups party, I don't want the ride to end.

But inevitably it does.

Trying my best to be silent, I drag myself up the stairs to my front door and open it with Simon's keys. I float through the living room, exhausted yet somehow contented. And over-joyed at the thought of collapsing into bed...

There's strangely satisfied feeling in my belly. To my surprise, it seems I'm already looking forward to playing pool with Action Man again next Saturday.

I pull on a big, black Nirvana t-shirt that's faded to charcoal and worn-in to butter soft (which I stole in a relationship settlement a few years ago...), turn on the fan at the end of my bed and slide in between my sheets.

As my head sinks into the pillow, I can feel myself already slipping away. The last thought through my head is one last Birthday wish...

A wish for sleep.

Deep, dreamless sleep...

He is waiting - not patiently.

His back is to the room.

His fingers drumming expectantly on a credenza.

It's a very expensive hotel room.

128

A huge bed with beautiful linen. A Louis XV sofa upholstered in pale blue silk. Thick oriental carpet.

A room service cart. A small, elegant dining setting for two. Flowers on the table.

The flowers!

Blood is suddenly thudding in my ears.

Air-brushed pink roses and lime hellebores...

My flowers!

That weird order I did today. What was the name...? Max Black...???

Oh fuck!

This is real.

An ice bucket, a seafood platter and some smoked salmon blinis are ready on the cart.

He is wearing beige trousers and a fine, white shirt - both immaculately pressed - a brown, patterned cravat and tan leather driving moccasins with no socks.

His hair is so pale it is almost colourless, barely strawberry blond and starting to grey.

His eyes gleam like a reptile.

The door opens.

He takes a deep breath and slowly turns.

The man from last night - the one waiting at the door - is dressed as a waiter. She is lead into the room and his tongue darts over his lips.

I shudder, repulsed, as my heart feels like it's going to explode in my chest.

She has been dressed in a chartreuse silk shift dress.

Expensive and elegant.

I am so terrified for her my stomach retches.

"Ah... well don't you look lovely?"

He gestures affably to the table.

"Please... have a seat."

She stands frozen. Unable to move.

"*Sit!*" he roars.

She stumbles to the chair which he has gallantly pulled out for her and sinks with unsteady knees as he slides it to the table.

He lingers over her.

Inhaling her.

Her smell and her fear.

"You've met Wolfgang of course...? He will be our waiter this evening. He is also very prepared and capable of subduing you, should you choose to be less than cooperative.... I know I repeat myself, but I must say you look remarkable in that dress - doesn't she, Wolfgang? Not many girls can wear that colour... Let us have champagne, Wolfgang. 1982 - for sentimental reasons, but it's also an excellent vintage."

She accepts the glass with a shaking hand.

Her eyes dart around the room, looking desperately for a way out. Every muscle trembling with fear.

She keeps her lips clamped together, trying to quell the lump that's building in her throat before it triggers tears.

Determined that they will not see her cry.

Oh God! Somebody help her!

"A votre santé!"

He raises his glass to her and takes a sip, all the time watching her. Relishing in her terror.

Wolfgang offers a blini. She gives her head a tiny shake.

"Take it and eat it!" he bellows at her.

With a shaking hand, she picks it up and brings it to her lips. Her mouth is dry with terror.

She tries to chew, but she can't form saliva. With difficulty, she swallows it and gulps some champagne to stop herself choking on it. He offers her another.

"Very good. Aren't they delicious...? May I offer you an oyster...? Don't chew, just suck and swallow... Good girl! Have another... *Have another!*"

His eyes narrow, his tongue darts out and licks the salty juice from his lips.

"So... my dear... now is when we play a game. You do like games, don't you? I love games..."

He slips his foot out of his shoe, sliding it across the plush carpet to meet her bare feet. He wriggles his big toe under her soft instep and caresses it.

Her whole body convulses.

Repulsed.

Terrified.

"Oh. Don't be like that..."

His lips smile, but his eyes are cold as his toe slides slowly up the inside of her leg.

Ankle...

Calf...

Knee...

"So... the game... You would like your freedom. I would like you - "

He pauses as his hand disappears below the table and in the agonising silence she can hear his trousers unzip.

And her heartbeat is crashing in her ears.

"I would like you to show me what you are prepared to do for your freedom..."

As his fat fingers reach over the table to trap her wrist in a vice-like grip, her stomach convulses and she jerks forward... projectile vomiting its contents everywhere.

The tablecloth, the dress, his shirt... all covered in bile, undigested food and still bubbling champagne.

A chunk of salmon clings to his cheek.

He sits frozen.

Horrified.

Then he springs out of his chair and backhands her across the face so hard it sends her flying out of her chair like a doll.

"*You fucking savage!*"

He roars like an animal.

He stands over her, shaking with rage.

"You fucking bitch. You've ruined everything. Wolfgang! She's ruined everything. Ruined my dress... ruined my night... ruined my favourite story..."

She hit her head on the cart on the way down.

She can't hear him.

She's unconscious.

"What would you like to do with her...?" Wolfgang asks hesitantly.

"I don't care what you do with her. Freeze her and feed her to the fucking sharks."

Petulant.

Like a spoilt child.

"This can all be fixed good as new..."

Talking the spoilt child down from his tantrum.

"Vomit is better than blood. It's bad when they bleed..."

"Yes..."

Absently.

Shaking his head.

134

Bitterly disappointed that he didn't get to play his game.

"Maybe a different story tomorrow night...?" Wolfgang suggests hopefully.

He looks up slowly, his pale eyes gleaming.

"Which... game...?"

"May I suggest we take her to the cinema?"

"Oh! Excellent, Wolfgang! *Excellent.*"

Sunday 9.15 am

A problem shared
Is a problem doubled.

There's loud banging and ringing.

I'm floating... numb... in nothingness...

And I want to keep floating...

But the banging and ringing are getting louder.

A voice is yelling my name.

"Cressida! *Sid!* Open the door!"

Vaguely it registers the voice is Simon.

Simon is apparently outside.

And I need to let him in... so the banging and yelling will stop.

I throw myself out of bed and try to stand up on very unsteady legs. My heart feels like I'm plummeting on a rollercoaster as my stomach pitches up into my mouth...

Here we go again...

Not good.

Really not good.

I stagger to the front door, open it a crack and the bright sunlight blinds me. Without even looking outside, hand over my eyes, I stumble back over to the sofa and sink down. Elbows on knees. Head in hands.

"Oh God! She's had another one! This is exactly what she was like yesterday."

I'm vaguely aware Simon must be speaking to someone, but it's such an effort just to hold vertical together that I can't bring myself to look up.

A body sits down carefully next to me and I know without looking it isn't Simon. Too much weight for his bird-like frame.

With my head still clutched in my hands, I can see a muscular thigh in very neat dark denim jeans.

I can smell leather, chocolate and...

I turn my head slightly sideways and somehow Action Man is sitting on my couch.

I pinch him on the thigh - hard - to make sure he's real. Then I pinch myself - hard - to make sure I'm not dreaming.

We both flinch, so I guess he is ...and I'm not.

I am apparently looking very confused, because Simon starts talking to me like English is my second language.

"Cressida, this is Mick... You met him last night, remember...? Mick is also a secret agent and he's here to interview you about the dreams."

I nod. Slowly and a little vaguely.

"Secret Agent...? So... you really *are* Action Man... hmmm... interesting..." I mutter softly, trying to work out if remaining upright is a possibility or if this spinning room is going to be the end of me. My head feels like it's not entirely stuck to my body and I can't stop the little waves of nausea that keep rising steadily from my guts.

Mick clears his throat awkwardly, then starts talking quietly and with calm authority. His Official Capacity voice.

"Cressida, I'm Michael O'Malley. I'm not a secret agent, I'm a federal intelligence officer. I want you to start at the beginning and tell me everything you saw - every detail, no matter how small or insignificant. If it gets too distressing, we can stop at any time. Okay?"

I nod vaguely.

Simon hovers in front of me.

"Can I get you something? Water...? Coffee...? *Pants...?!*"

"Bring her tea with a lot of sugar. It should help."

And he's staring at me intently again.

"Carlisle... ? Are you related to - "

"Gordon Carlisle...? I'm his daughter."

"Good to know - " he mutters. Dad is the kind of high profile barrister that makes law enforcement uncomfortable... "- but I was going to say Delia."

"Yes. She's my grandma."

The thought of her makes me smile weakly. I turn a little more to face him. His strong features remind me of a lion. Last night's two day growth is now a very rugged three. His face is taut and his eyes are dark with fatigue. Up this close, I notice the faintest suggestion of a crescent-shaped scar high on his left cheekbone.

And my head has now finally got it together to the point where I realise I am sitting next to a strange man basically naked, but for Josh Gillespie's Nirvana t-shirt.

He frowns.

"I'd always been a skeptic. Thought it was bullshit. A few years ago I was on a case... a little girl vanished and we had *nothing*. And we were running out of time. Someone suggested we call in Delia... She presented a line of enquiry we hadn't considered and in one hour we had it cracked open. So if you're Delia Carlisle's granddaughter, if you're talking, I'm going to listen."

"Can I ask you a question?"

Something has been bothering me.

He nods, earnestly.

"Do you iron your jeans? They look...far... too neat..."

"Errr... yes. I do," he frowns, looking quite bemused.

I nod gravely.

"Hmmmm... interesting..."

Simon puts a mug that offers the helpful advice *You Already Know That And I Don't Care* in my hand. I automatically take a sip, then splutter it everywhere.

"That's disgusting!" I splutter. However the warm mug feels comforting, so I clamp both hands around it and start talking.

A black leather sofa.

Red running shoes.

Just taking Bear for a run...

I'm on autopilot. The words keep rolling out of my mouth in a flat monotone. Staring down into the sickly sweet tea the whole time...

Nightmare Number One. Every disturbing detail. Start to finish.

Nightmare Number Two. Every disturbing detail. Start to finish.

I don't know how long I've talked for, but by the time I'm done my knuckles are white and the mug is stone cold.

I turn to him very slowly.

"Do you believe me...?"

"I don't disbelieve you."

Suddenly I remember Bear.

"Did you find the dog?"

"Yes. He was badly dehydrated and needed multiple surgeries, but he should make it."

My heart goes cold. Anxiety slowly, steadily escalating to panic.

"*You have to find her!*"

I blurt it out. I know I'm shrieking but I can't stop it. My tone is frantic.

"*He is a monster.*"

He asks questions about the Max Black flower order... most of which I can't answer - it was ordered on-line and left in the shop to be collected. No actual contact. No delivery address. And I'm even less helpful with the tech related questions... I haven't a clue about platforms and servers.

Then he shows me a photo on his phone.

142

"Do you know this girl?"

I suck my breath in.

It's her.

"Who is she?"

She is a foreign student studying Medicine at Melb Uni. Her father is ambassador to Australia from a political hot potato country. Her mother's family are obscenely wealthy industrialists.

"You've never met her...?"

"No. Why would I...?"

"Your sister is enrolled at Melbourne University in the same year..."

I snort.

"Larry may be enrolled, but it's questionable whether she actually goes there... And even if she did, she'd be hanging with the Private School Party Girls - she has nothing in common with an Asian med student. I've never met her - never set eyes on her - before I saw her in the dreams... And this isn't helping her! *You have to find her! Now!*"

"We're waiting for the ransom call. She's been kidnapped and someone will make demands. Either money or some political concession."

I stare at him for a long time, frowning.

"You're wrong. It's not that at all. The only thing he wants is to play with her and kill her."

Mick is incredulous.

"So you're saying this is just a crime of opportunity? Not possible. All that motive and she was just in the wrong place at the wrong time...? It doesn't add up. Cressida, this is what we do. We know what we're talking about."

"You have no idea what you're talking about! If you wanted to kidnap her, would you really be driving round in a van after midnight in case she just happened to feel like going for a run??? *That doesn't add up.*"

My voice sounds too loud and borderline hysterical in my ears.

"*For fuck's sake!* We don't have time to be arguing about this! You need to listen to me!"

He's not happy and I get the feeling he's not used to being told what to do, but he must know I have a point because he changes the subject.

"Where do you think they're holding her? Can you give me anything more? Anything at all?"

I sigh in frustration.

144

"It feels... somehow familiar, but I can't quite put my finger on it. There's something weird about the atmosphere... and there's something about the way voices sound in her cell... I know what it is, but I can't quite..."

My phone starts ringing and I'm about to ignore it when Simon falls over himself to get it to me in time, shoving it in my face.

I look at the caller and frown.

"Marco? Why would Marco be calling me...?"

Simon is so excited he's jiggling like a Christmas elf and he can't get the word out of his mouth quickly enough.

"BABY!!!"

"Oh shit! Baby!"

I pick up the call just in time.

"Get here. Get here right now." Marc sounds uncharacteristically grim and panic-stricken.

"What's wrong? Please tell me everything's okay?"

I've read the Birth Plan. All eighty pages of it. And as far as I can remember, I am not required until Post Birth - 'Cressida to coordinate flower and gift deliveries'.

"You have to get down here *now*! She's lost it - *totally lost it...* You're the only one who can talk her down. *Please!*"

"On my way. Meet me in the lobby."

Mick has been talking in a low voice on his phone the whole time I've been talking to Marc.

"You gotta go somewhere...? I can give you a ride and we can keep talking on the way..."

"Okay. But y'all need to stop thinking it's a kidnapping - you've got it wrong and she's going to die if you don't figure it out - soon!"

The Girl Who Cried Wolfe

Marco is pacing the hospital lobby, looking at his phone every five seconds, all but tearing out his hair.

"Oh thank God!"

He drags me into the lift and we go up to her room.

"What the hell is going on?"

He just shakes his head.

"I've never seen her like this before... She's always so in control... so perfect. Calm. Kind. Capable. Rational... Man! *She's fucking snapped!*"

We're standing in front of a closed door. He opens it and shoves me in.

My explodingly pregnant sister is calmly and quietly packing her bag.

Yes.

I said *packing*.

Every five-star rated, eco-friendly, organic, yummy-mummy item of clothing, cosmetic, baby-care (and those weird baby-having gadgets I don't know anything about...) are being carefully removed from the drawers and wardrobes - where they'd been not so long ago carefully arranged - and placed carefully back into Miranda's Louis Vuitton overnight bag.

"Watcha doin'...?" I ask cautiously, because yes. All evidence *is* pointing to the fact that she has indeed fucking lost it.

She replies with disturbing calmness.

"I'm sorry but this was a really bad idea."

When I don't reply, she looks up from a pile of organic Japanese nappies and says like it's the most reasonable conclusion in the world...

"I'm not doing this. It was a bad idea. I'm going home now."

"I'm not so sure that's an option..."

"Nup. Not doing it - *Aaaaaarrrggghhh!*"

She gasps, doubling over in pain while clutching that ripe belly.

Suddenly I'm feeling quite alarmed and a bit useless.

Should we be timing this or something...?

"Miranda. The baby has to come out."

"That's the fucking problem!"

She's yelling at me, suddenly snapping into hysterical, panic-stricken mode.

"I've just realised there's only one way it's coming out and no! *I'm not doing that!*"

Fascinating as it is to see the Model Child unravelling for the first time in her life, I don't know a lot about having babies, but I do know the clock is ticking.

"It's normal to be scared but I'm sure you'll be -"

"*Fine...? Are you about to say fine???*"

She is shrieking like a mad woman.

Her classically beautiful face is red and contorted in frantic hysteria.

"I don't see you signing up to push a fucking watermelon through your cervix. Do you know what an episiotomy is...???"

I take a deep breath and...

Bang!

I slap her so hard across her left cheek I can see the imprint of my hand. She stares at me, frozen, and for a second I think she's going to hit me back. Then her bottom lip starts quivering and she dissolves into tears.

"I'm so scared. I don't like this feeling at all. I don't think I can do it."

And I reach around the giant, time-bomb belly and hug her, kissing her on the cheek, my heart swelling.

"There's nothing you can't do, Golden Girl."

I laugh softly, gently wiping away a tear with my thumb.

To my relief, she starts laughing too.

"You're in the best place. You're in good hands, I'm sure you've done all your homework ... Now go lie down... or kneel down... or whatever the hell you do... and have that beautiful baby."

She takes a deep breath and looks me right in the eye. Conspiratorially.

"Yep. Nobody needs to know about this. Your secret is safe with me... Hey, for a moment, I thought you were going to hit me back..."

"Oh I thought about it all right..." she giggles, then gently pulls me as close as her big belly will allow and whispers "Love you like a rainbow!"

"Ditto!" I whisper back.

And I walk out the door, holding my hand up to tag team Marco.

"Crisis averted. You're on, Dad! - oh! She had a contraction while I was in there, like in the middle maybe, if that's important..."

Marco nods and half-smiles.

Nervous and distracted.

I squeeze his shoulder.

"Good luck! She's got this!"

As the lift doors open, I walk in, about to text Simon. I am not too proud to beg for a ride home...

"Of all the elevators, in all the hospitals, in all the world... she walks into mine."

I'd know that voice anywhere.

Deep and resonant.

Rich, smooth and sticky like golden syrup.

If you don't already know it, you're about to find out that Melbourne is a very small town...

I look up from my phone to see familiar grey eyes taking me in exactly the same way as when I first bumped into them about ten years ago.

Languid. Suggestive. A bit bored, a bit amused, and a bit something I've never quite been able to figure out. His face is a little older, taut with stress and exhaustion. Same handsome features. Same Jesus-like facial hair.

Oh Saturn! You have got to be fucking joking.

We met at Debating Society. He was in his final year of Medicine, I was in my first week of Law. Those grey eyes prowled lazily over my body, from my eyes to my toes. I went from Zero to Major Crush in sixty seconds. It turned into a far too long, one-sided saga that was never going to have a happy ending. Not the first girl to make that mistake... and I won't be the last.

After acknowledging me with a cheeky raised eyebrow, his eyes start slowly mentally undressing me.

Dr Jamie Wolfe.

His tallish, more grown-up but still lanky frame looking very at home in jeans and a faded almost beyond recognition music festival t-shirt. He must have just finished a shift.

We didn't have a Relationship. We have History.

It never should have made it past the pilot, yet it became a mini series that went on for *way* too many seasons. I was his Booty Call when he didn't have a better offer. It took four years for me to figure out that answering the call wasn't going to magically transform me into his Girlfriend. Yes. I like to learn the hard way...

Not the first girl to make that mistake either, right...?

For him, old habits apparently die hard...

By the way he's looking at me now, I'm expecting to be propositioned in three... two... o-

"You're looking... good... "

He says it slowly. Every word weighted with our rollercoaster past... fateful present... and the hopeful possibility of an immediate future.

Leaving in a tremendous hurry, I threw on the first thing I could find in my panic to get here. A (very!) short turquoise and orange print boho-chic sundress.

Low neckline, little puffy sleeves, ruffle around the hem... and little buttons all the way up the front. Can't help but chuckle at the irony... all the time I wasted plotting to 'accidentally' bump into him when he mattered so desperately... now it happens without even trying after not giving him a thought for, what...? How many years...???

"Are you mentally unbuttoning me from the top... or the bottom...?"

He tosses his long, dark auburn hair and laughs darkly.

153

"You know me too well. The bottom... So... are you doing anything right now? Can I take you for a drink?"

"Is that a euphemism?"

"I was thinking more of a prelude..."

"A prelude to what...?" with wide-eyed innocence, whilst knowing exactly what he has in mind.

"Us getting... reacquainted..."

Whislt I have absolutely no intention of reacquainting myself with the very talented Dr Wolfe, he's holding car keys. I'm guessing it won't be to hard to get him to drive me home...

"My place...? I think I have beer..."

Specifically I think *Simon* has beer, but let's not allow pesky questions of ownership to get in the way of a free ride...

The corners of his mouth are slowly curling into a naughty smile.

"God I've missed you."

Can't help it. I laugh.

"I seriously doubt that, Doctor Wolfe."

His brow furrows almost imperceptibly as he feels the paradigm shift... the tables turn... and the rug maybe about to be pulled out from under him.

154

Doors open into the basement carpark and a steamy wall of heat and exhaust fumes hit us. There, in the Doctor Parking section, is a familiar baby blue vintage VW Beetle.

"Omg! You've still got that car!"

"And you still apparently have *no* car..."

"Which ward are you on...? Please don't say Ob/Gyn..." I shoot him an alarmed sidelong glance.

"I'm specialising in Neurology. Strokes... trauma... It's pretty humbling. How about you? You've finished, yeah...? Being a good girl in the family business...?"

Involuntarily I pull a face at the funky old-car-on-a-hot-day smell... and at the question. With a sigh I ease myself onto the red, cracked vinyl seat. I have a bit of a seatbelt-neckline-cleavage situation, and I don't have to look to know he'll be captivated by it. *Sigh* So predictable... He's frozen, hand on key, key in ignition. Then he drags his focus back to the task at hand. With a cough and a splutter the engine turns over and we pull out into the blindingly bright day.

"I dropped out. I'm a florist now."

Despite the fact that the car is now moving, he turns to stare at me.

"You're a *what???* You're not serious! - oh hey! What were you doing at St Francis'...?"

Phew! Off the hook.

"Miranda's having a baby."

"Miranda is...?"

"My perfect big sister. Degree, career, wedding, husband, house. Now she's ticking off Baby..."

"Ah! And how's your list going?" he asks with a smirk.

"I have not even managed to succeed in the writing of the list..." I giggle.

"Boyfriend...?"

"Nope. Can't say I've got any better at that. Still hopelessly attracted to bad boys who don't love me back while breaking the hearts of sweet, responsible boys who I'd probably be much better off with... You...?"

"Same same. Good girls bore me. Bad girls treat me as badly as I treat them. And one girl is never enough."

He laughs. An easy, open, throaty, sexy laugh.

"So looks like we're still made for each other."

156

"I would seriously question we were *ever* made for each other..."

It's an easy ten minute drive through Melbourne's big, green parks, around the MCG and over the river to South Yarra.

"Oh nice! When was this built? Thirties...? Is this a Howard Lawson building...?" he exclaims as we pull up out the front.

Now despite being a philandering rat, he does have a very sexy mind that can intelligently discuss pretty much anything... Hmmmm... perhaps this is actually instrumental to his success as a philandering rat...

I lead the way up the stairs, suspecting that his eyes are trained on the little ruffle at the bottom of my dress, hoping for a glimpse of inner thigh with every step.

"Great space! Who else lives here...?" he says as he looks around the living room, following me into the kitchen to the fridge.

"I share with a guy called Simon..." I call over my shoulder.

"And Simon is gay." Jamie pronounces matter-of-factly.

"Really? Is that wishful thinking...?"

"No. That is a general observation. This is *far* too stylish and tidy for anyone but a gay man..."

I open the door and see a six-pack right down on the bottom shelf. Sorry Simon! I'll replace it... Promise!

As I bend over, I suspect that the hemline is going to ride up...

I turn back to Jamie, holding two bottles of beer.

"You just tried to see my butt then, didn't you...?" I narrow my eyes at him suspiciously.

"Sorry not sorry..." as he raises a cheeky eyebrow at me.

I lead him through the living room out onto the private balcony. Original 1930's tiles, a beautiful view over the Yarra river to the Melbourne CBD, afternoon sun and a rattan two-seat sofa.

We sit. He stretches out his lean limbs, knocks back some beer and closes his eyes, feeling the sun on his face.

It looks like the first time he's sat down all day.

I kick off my Birkenstocks and sit sideways like I always do. My orange toenails are almost touching his thigh.

"It was noted that you didn't answer my question, Cressida... What happened?"

I sigh.

"Well... I went to Oxford..."

"Yes. You left me. I imagined you bewitching a Lord with a silly name and ending up Lady of the Manor."

"He was an Earl and his name was Tolly - short for Bartholomew..."

"*Shit!* You're not joking, are you?"

"Nope. I panicked and ran away. He was so... earnest... like a Labrador... He was wasted on me then - I didn't want kind and sweet... I wanted-"

"Bad boys..."

"Actually I was going to say *assholes*..."

"Ouch!" he winces theatrically. "Harsh!... But why'd you chuck your degree? You were brilliant... well-connected..." he lowers his eyes and adds quietly "...beautiful. You could have - "

"I could have ended up working twice as hard for half the credit in the sexist Boy's Club with a pack of wankers who think winning the game is more important than doing the right thing."

"I'm guessing that's *not* how you explained it to your family..."

"You chose medicine. You wanted to be a doctor. No one ever asked me! They asked if I was smart enough to read law... if I was clever enough to argue law... but nobody ever asked if I actually *wanted* to do it. And I never even asked myself..."

I take a long swig of beer.

I'm not looking at him, but I can feel those grey eyes on my face.

"It was the Tolly thing that pushed me over the edge."

His eyes narrow.

You have no right to be jealous, Mister.

His fingers start playing absently with my toes.

"It was a hoot to start with... parties, polo, country houses... and his family were absolutely gorgeous...but I had never even considered marriage and nobody seemed to notice that being their Breath of Fresh Air was suffocating me..."

I gulp some more beer.

"So when he presented me with an extremely large diamond ring, I ran screaming... but we were in a hedge maze at the time, so I ended up hopelessly fucking lost and literally trapped- *Stop laughing! It's not funny!* - I never wanted to hurt him, but I just panicked." I sigh and look away, remembering Tolly's handsome face looking so hurt and bewildered... and I flashback to Simon, last night... *Fraidy Cat! Fraidy Cat!*

Taking a big mouthful of beer, I shake my head to dislodge the memory of both. I continue.

160

"I'd met an Aussie guy at a party... Simon... He was working as a stylist for UK Vogue. We clicked instantly. I sent him an SOS. He moved me into his flat, sat me down and for the first time in my life someone actually asked me what made me happy. And the first thing I thought of was flowers... So he found me a job. And I found I was really good at it."

"And eventually you had to come home with some explaining to do..."

I shift uncomfortably in my seat.

Yes. I did and it wasn't pretty. Because I *may or may not* have neglected to inform them I'd dropped out... There was shock. Then there was disappointment. Then there was *It's just a phase you're going through...* - which couldn't help but feel dismissive or condescending... and I couldn't quite work out which was more offensive...

Until we finally, eventually, arrived at acceptance.

It wasn't fun the first time round, and I have absolutely no desire to relive it.

All this poking around is making me increasingly uncomfortable. Poking around at broken things, trying to identify the problem, is however what Doctor Jamie does for a living. Especially when something doesn't quite make sense...

I throw my head back to get the last of the beer out of my bottle, wipe my lips with the back of my hand and make some meaningful eye contact.

"Are you going to continue with this vivisection, because if you are I'm going to need another beer..."

He shakes his head.

"I'm trying to process how you could just throw everything away... Bad decision after bad decision..."

In my head I hear Simon's voice...*terrible choices... terrible choices...* as I pad barefoot to the kitchen.

"That's ironic coming from you... possibly my worst decision..." I yell back at him, slamming the fridge door.

He winces theatrically as I reappear before him, with beers.

"Harsh!"

"True!" as I clink necks to Cheers! him, before upending the bottle into my mouth. He's staring at me, brow slightly furrowed. Processing.

162

"I'm sure we can think of something better to talk about than me-"

"But I still don't understand... all those years... all that work... just-"

He's not going to give up, is he...? I can only think of one way to shut him up...

I take the bottle out of his hand and swinging a leg over his thighs, deposit myself in his lap.

And kiss him.

Hard.

For a split second he does nothing.

Then his mouth opens a little wider and he slowly kisses me back. Muscle memory kicks in, causing some fluttering and vague longing. He is a damn good kisser, and seriously, I cannot even remember the last time anybody kissed me seriously.

We come up for air and he traces a lazy finger along my calf up to my knee.

"Thought I was - quote- *Possibly your worst decision...*?"

"Oh yes! You are. One could go as far as to say *Unquestionably*, even..."

"*Unquestionably...?!*" He raises a cheeky eyebrow..

"Yes," nodding as I lean forward to gently hook my fingers through his hair and push it back behind his ear, "Unquestionably... oh! Hang on..."

I wrinkle my nose. Tough call...

"Actually you get to share the title of Worst Decision..."

"With whom...?" his naughty grey eyes narrow in mock suspicion.

"Nobody you know..."

"Indulge me."

"Bad Boy East London chef. I broke Tolly's heart, then he broke mine... That's Karma for you, right...?"

His brow furrows thoughtfully as his grey eyes search my face.

"You've changed. You're different."

"How so?"

"More confident. Less needy. I like it."

Hmmmm... too little, too late as far as I'm concerned. However I have a horrible feeling he's going to keep wanting to dissect me. And I've already over-shared.

So I stare hard at his lips.

"Is it possible for you to just kiss me???" I ask almost in a whisper.

"Oh it's entirely possible," he almost whispers back, smirking. "Would you like me to...?"

"Yes. Yes, I would!"

"Why didn't you just say...?"

Slowly and very deliberately, he lets his lips melt into mine. His hands slide up my back, reacquainting themselves with my topography. Hormones try to engage auto-pilot, however my brain argues a reprise of greatest hits and memories with Doctor Jamie is going to be another terrible, terrible decision. Right...?

So just as I'm trying to figure out how to make my lips and tongue cut it out, when they really, really don't want to stop-

"Cressida! Sid! Where are you? Are you here?"

The door is flung open and there is Simon.

"Oh!"

Now... this is where most people quickly and quietly close the door, at least a little uncomfortable if not embarrassed. But not my Simon!... and he carries on... completely unbothered by the fact that he's just walked in on two people doing as much as they can with all their clothes on. He looks at Jamie pointedly and a little confused.

Then he sits down on the sofa, extending his hand.

"Hi! I'm Simon!" he pronounces chirpily.

Jamie frowns slightly, his grey eyes saying *What the actual fuck...?...* before reaching over to receive Simon's handshake and introduce himself.

I'm laughing and shaking my head.

"You get used to it. I've chosen to find it charming."

"Is there a baby...?" Simon asks expectantly.

"Ideally not..." Jamie mutters darkly.

I glance over at my phone.

"Nope. Not yet..."

Then Simon turns his attention back to Jamie.

"So... how do we know you?"

"This is *Doctor* Jamie."

Simon makes a silent *Oh!* with his lips, leaving no doubt that he has heard all about Cressida And Jamie - When Love Goes Wrong.

"He works at St Francis'... I bumped into him in the lift..."

"Hmmmm... apparently! " with a raised eyebrow.

"Is there something I can help you with???"

I try to sound pointed, but I start to dissolve into giggles as I attempt removing myself gracefully from Jamie's lap. And fail spectacularly.

"Yes... no... maybe... oh I don't remember... *This* is much more interesting... So, Sid... did you...?"

And he lowers his gaze to Jamie's crotch.

"No. No I did not."

"Oh that's a shame. We could have used some feedback..."

Jamie turns to look at me quizzically.

I look down, smoothing my eyebrow, because I know what's coming next.

"I've been coaching her... levelling up certain skills..."

Jamie raises a sly eyebrow at me.

"Perhaps next time..."

"It's cute how you assume there's going to be a next time..."

And Doctor Jamie is, for once, quite speechless.

And then Simon starts jumping up and down on the spot and clapping his hands... which means he's remembered why he barged in here...

"- oh! That's right! Do you ever check your messages...? Everyone's going for drinks at Karmageddon for your Birthday hmmmm..." - looking at his watch - "... pretty much now.... You need to hit the shower - you stink!"

This is when I remember that I left in such a hurry this morning, I most likely *do* stink...

"Can you find me something to wear...? Pretty please???"

I glance over at Jamie. Unaccustomed to not being the most important person in the room, he looks like he's contemplating the meaning of irony.

Hmmm... awkward...

"I'm not invited, am I...?"

A little wistfully, I think back to wide-eyed little First Year me... how many hours she wasted waiting for him to call... how desperately she hoped one day he'd want to make her his girlfriend... how many tears she cried every time she dared to consider the probability that was never going to happen.

This ones for you, Kiddo!

"Ah... *No!*" I bend down and give him a peck on the cheek. "Good to see you! Thanks for the ride..."

"I could make a house call - should you ever find yourself having an emergency..."

"Good to know!" I nod politely.

"Ummm... I'm pretty sure you don't have my number..."

So apparently the trait he finds most alluring is disinterest. With a vague *Oh!*, I throw my phone at him and scoot off to make myself ready to face Karmageddon.

Simon and I are standing on the street in the late afternoon sun, waiting for our Uber. It's still ridiculously hot for April, but the sky is starting to cloud over and you can feel something brewing in the air.

A cold front is on the way and the temperature will drop fifteen degrees almost instantly. Welcome to Melbourne! Four seasons in one day... When that front hits this high pressure system, there's going to be the mother of all thunder storms.

Simon - in a rare moment of seriousness - has asked me what's going on. And I reply a very honest *Absolutely nothing.*

Except for the tiny, self-satisfied smile on my face that Karma may have just avenged my poor, wronged little eighteen-year-old self, all other traces of Jamie have been washed down the plug-hole.

Simon's dressed me in a denim mini - which he pronounced 'not short enough' as we were about to walk out the door, so he took to it with a pair of scissors - and loaned me a black muscle tank with armholes split almost to my waist, so there's a little flash of leopard print bra every time I move.

He found some big, turquoise earrings from Gran I'd forgotten I owned in my jewellery box, and while he would have preferred a more dramatic footwear choice, conceded that 'with my coordination skills' the leopard Birkenstocks were a better OHS option if I was drinking. My hair's still wet, but it should be drip-dried by the time we get there, and I managed to preserve the leftovers of Danh's eyeliner, shadow and mascara - which I realise is probably not hygienic, but it's a whole lot better than I can do.

One of life's great mysteries is... how does Simon always look so good...? Despite fleetingly sleeping (I'm guessing last night he had none), rarely eating, never exercising and subsisting on a diet of caffeine, cocktails and Marlboro Lights, he always looks bright-eyed, well-rested and fit. He's trying to suck down a quick cigarette before our car gets here, his hair turning gold in the sunlight.

Black t-shirt, perfectly worn jeans, snake print thongs, a studded leather cuff on one wrist and rockstar sunglasses.

Climbing into the car, Simon asks me to set a reminder on my phone.

"I put a load of your washing in, you lazy bitch! If you put it in the dryer when we get home, you'll actually have clothes for tomorrow."

I pull my phone out, remembering I should also be checking for a Baby Update...

What appears on the screen takes me so much by surprise it makes me gasp.

A little wave of sentiment for Little Lost Me... a pragmatic too much/too little/too late from Present Me... and an unprecedented parting glance at Doctor Jamie with his guard down.

Simon's hand is on my knee and his beautiful cornflower blue eyes are wide with alarm and concern.

"What???"

And I show him.

A white screen, arranged with neatly arranged rows of little black words.

Lyrics.

Bob Dylan.

You're A Big Girl Now.

A *Calamity* of Cocktails...

If you're not up on your Hindi mythology, you won't find Karma-geddon... But first you have to find the right dead-end bluestone cobbled laneway in between the right historic red brick buildings that all kinda look the same... Yep. Welcome to Melbourne.

Your only clue is a twelve foot tall mural of Kali the Destroyer.

Even if you don't know who she is, she immediately catches your eye in the (literally!) wall-to-wall rainbow of graffiti art. Props to whoever's head she came out of - it's talent to take something so horrifically violent and make it sexy... sassy... *charming* even...

She guards the huge double doors, with her ten iridescent baby blue arms holding her arsenal of weapons - the scimitar, the knife, the trident... all dripping with blood - plus a severed male head which she's holding rather thoughtfully by his long hair. (And like any good, resourceful woman, she's catching the drips in a shallow dish for future use.)

Despite her demonic eyes, carnivorous teeth and fluorescent red pointy tongue, there's something almost cute about her heart-shaped face and heart-shaped lips. Her necklace of skulls doesn't entirely obscure her spectacular little breasts - curvy, buoyant and perfect. Impossibly teeny waist gives way to sexy hips and capable quads that sport a mini skirt made from bright green feathers... and dismembered human arms. She wears a huge, bejewelled head dress. Her long, strong limbs are adorned with elaborate gold cuffs and chains.

I give her a little wave as Simon gallantly opens the door for me, grabbing what at first glance appears to be the handle of her knife.

"Oh hello!" I say to the lime green cobra that's curled around the base of her trident. I've never noticed him before.

We begin the trek up seven floors of stairs. The bluestone steps have been worn smooth over the decades by millions of feet.

After the cool, dark, drab stairwell nothing can prepare you for the assault on your senses when the doors open before you to Karmageddon.

Taking its cue from a Rajasthani palace, every surface - walls, ceiling, floor - is a riot of texture and colour. Murals by the same hand that created Kali cover the walls and ceiling - a cheeky twist on traditional Indian art. At first glance you notice the hunting and warrior scenes... then you do a little *oh!* as you realise that interspersed with the Maharani portraits and men with spears on horseback are depictions of the more creative positions of the Kama Sutra.

As well as partying here to abandonment on more than one occasion, I've done flowers for more than a few functions here. Every time I notice something new in the intricate, clever design. I also know a few of the staff, which could come in handy if the bar is as busy as I suspect it will be. It's pretty thirsty weather.

We make our way through the inside bar, with its elaborate, tessellated and painted columns, huge upholstered couches and wild, oriental carpets; and head out to the rooftop. It's virtually empty in here, save for a few unhappy-looking groups who got here too late to grab some real estate outside. Unlike Simon's crew, who were either early or lucky enough to score pole position - the two giant carved wooden day beds right on the corner of the balcony with a huge, matching coffee table in the middle.

About a dozen cool-looking people have languidly draped themselves over the couches and table. There's a lot of black, denim, ethnic prints, straw hats or baseball caps and seriously fuck-off expensive sunglasses. And speaking of which... I see Danh notice Simon about to walk through the door and he takes his sunglasses off... then puts them back on again... then takes them off again. Mr Cool is nervous fidgeting! *Ooh errrr!!!* I realise with a little pang of guilt that I've been so caught up in myself, I haven't even asked Simon about last night...

Two depleted pitchers of Mojitos - their ice almost melted - and a couple of picked-over platters of samosa-looking things sit on the table. From the rowdiness surrounding the table, I'm guessin' they're not on their first round and I'm thinking that it's also a fair bet that most of them are still kicking on from last night.

There's a lot of whooping and raised glasses as they see Simon and me appear. We wave enthusiastic *Hellos!*

"Ima gonna get us another round..." I say, a few steps out, before turning to head to the bar.

Now... the bar is not merely a bar... It's tiled like a palatial swimming pool, and has an actual waist-deep above ground pool attached that's surrounded by bar stools. Apparently no-one is quite drunk enough for a dip yet, but I'm guessing that won't be far off...

It's crazy busy and people are waiting three-deep the entire length of the bar. This is no fun at all... I'm getting hotter and thirstier (and more than a little shitty-kitty as a blonde Bar Bitch who I don't recognise overlooks me once again, when I'm pretty sure I'm next in line) ...when I feel a finger tickle my waist through the deep armhole of Simon's tank top. I spin around - ready to hug someone I know or hit someone I don't - to see a handsome hipster smiling down at me.

"Flower Girl! Thought that was you..."

Plush lips, a kind smile and perfect teeth. Dark brown eyes and matching hair twisted up into a man bun. Neatly manscaped facial hair completes the sun-kissed, boyishly handsome face.

Diego...

Karmageddon's Chilean bar manager. Given he's wearing cut-off jeans - and only cut-off jeans - I'm guessing he's not working today.

Like the rest of Ash Knight's veritable United Nations of staff, he's hot, hip and highly charming. And given he's looking more than a little worse for wear, I'm guessing there was some hard partying at The Wedding last night.

"So what brings the Flower Girl out to play...?"

His accent gives him the faintest lisp, which is really quite disarming.

"Birthday drinks. Mine!"

"Oh... hang on... I've got you. Where are you sitting? Over with Jimmy Quan and Simon Huxtable...?"

He puts his thumb and forefinger between his lips, resulting in an ear-splitting dog whistle.

"Hey! Phoebe! Two mojito jugs and some samosa for table twelve. *Now please...*"

Inwardly I smile.

Suck on that, Phoebe!

"Thank you!" I reach into my bra to pull out my card (I didn't have anywhere else to put it...) and Diego's eyes follow my hand. He laughs, shaking his head. His expression says *Really...?* His South American charm lets him tread the fine line between professional and flirty, nimble as a cat.

"Really! I seriously did not have anywhere else to put it!"

"Well you can put it back... in there... because this is on me Flower-Stroke-Birthday Girl."

He reaches easily over me, grabbing a pitcher in each hand then leads the way our corner.

Smoothly he pours two glasses, handing one to me then clinking his against it. *Cheers!*

"Happy Birthday, Flower Girl!"

Everyone at our table - and all the tables in the immediate vicinity - raises their glass and yells Happy Birthday at me. I can feel my face flushing with embarrassment. It's a lot more attention than I'm comfortable with. So I blurt out the first thing that comes into my head.

"Do you know who drew the Kali and the murals up here...?"

"Why do yo ask...?"

"I think they're amazing!"

I pause, waiting for him to say something, but he seems to want me to keep talking.

"To be so graphic and sexy, but so individual and...*charming* at the same time..."

And he's still not saying anything, so I blurt out -

"And the breasts are fabulous. Whoever did them has a very strong appreciation of boobs..."

"Oh... I do..." he replies softly.

"You...?"

Then I look closely at the tattoo that trails from his left bicep across his heart to his sternum.

Intricate Incan... deities, a condor, red trumpet-shaped flowers that look like a Christmas lily... a little more serious in tone, but the same intricate detail and charm. Absently I reach up and almost touch the out-stretched airborne front paws of the spectacular snarling puma about to leap right off Diego's well-defined left pectoral...

"Oh... of course! What's the flower...?"

"Chilean Bellflower..." He pronounces Chile with a soft *sh* sound... "and yes... I'm an illustrator. But this pays better for now... And yes. I love breasts..." he raises an eyebrow and smiles like a naughty boy. "Ash has asked me to do another one... I want to do the Trapeze - she's on her back and upside down, so if there isn't enough they'll disappear... I need to find a bit more than a good handful...hmmmm... actually like those..."

And after feeling more or less invisible for a very long time, I once again have the attention of an attractive man. I've somehow become a freaking Boy Magnet since... yesterday? Is this part of Nan's *After Midnight* prediction...??? Because if this is what a Return of Saturn is like, I'm seriously wondering why everyone complains about it - however contemplating my astrological predicament is interrupted by a squeal and a loud splash.

A tall girl with long, muscular limbs surfaces in the pool, laughing as she pulls off big, black sunglasses to wipe the water from her eyes. Long dark plaits, heart-shaped face and heart-shaped lips. One arm, and the opposite leg, covered in a spectacular Asian-inspired black line floral tattoo. Her red and black striped AC Milan jersey - so tight & tiny it looks like she stole it from a ten year-old boy - is now clinging to her seriously enviable boobs and tiny, tight waist.

"Oh my God! It's Kali!!!"

A smile of absolute child-like wonder spreads over my face.

"Well spotted." he laughs. "That's my wife, Jess."

And the beautiful thing is, with his ever-so-slight lisp, nobody in the whole world will say her name quite like him. He looks at her with completely unabashed love, pride and admiration.

"She's a personal trainer - she makes grown men cry for a living. You should see what she does to Ash...! She was born to be our Kali... Whoever pushed her in the pool had better be able to run...!"

"Oh Diego! She's..."

My voice trails off, because I can't find a word for how beautiful and magnificent she is... I have a kinda sad, wistful moment where I wish that for once I had someone who looked at me like that... and that I had rippley abs like that... or any abs at all, even...

"Yep." he says quietly, with a proud smile. "She's all that. She did some work with GGInc - they've built a game character on her... Can't you just see her slaying dragons and kicking ass...?"

Yes. I can. I can also see her spectacular boobies and glorious butt keeping a lot of little - and not-so-little - boys awake at night...

"Better find a towel for Jessie... but I'll find you later... to talk shop..."

"Shop...? You need flowers...?"

"The Trapeze! I think you're my girl..."

And with a wink, he disappears... and I turn my attention to my crew.

Technically, it's Simon's crew.

Simon collects people.

Like he collected me.

His enthusiasm for pretty much everything and rare ability to find anybody fascinating, making them feel like they're the only person in the world, means he collects new best friends like a highly sociable three year-old.

He's sitting perched on the carved wooden arm of the daybed, surrounded by people he's worked with or had random, chance

182

encounters with. Mostly it's a very Fashion crowd - stylists, designers, photographers, PR girls, hairdressers. Today's anomaly is Eloise, the accountant, who he once sat next to on a Sydney-to-Melbourne flight. Petite, dark wavy hair and cheeky dimples when she smiles. She's taken to introducing herself as a Creative Accountant because she said she started feeling kinda boring along side the rest of Team Simon.

I notice with a sly grin that he's perched next to Danh, and both of them are enjoying the excuse to be close together as they scroll through Danh's phone. They're all trawling the pics from last night's wedding.

I take a second to check for a Baby Update on mine.

Bah! Still no news...

"Jimmy! *Money Shot!!!*" Simon calls out, sweetly familiar as he turns Danh's hand around to show the photo on the screen...

Angelica is running down the wide, bluestone steps of St Michael's Cathedral, glancing back over her shoulder like Cinderella with the Disney princess dress billowing behind her.

Aha!

So the princess dress is Jimmy Quan's baby.

"Oh that's gold!" Jimmy looks like a proud new father. "And I could kiss whoever did the flowers. They're so fucking perfect."

"Turn around and pucker up!" Simon gestures over Jimmy's shoulder. "She's right behind you!"

Slowly he turns to look. When he sees me, he shakes his head and laughs as he kneels up on the sofa to wrap his hands around my face, planting a big, theatrical MWAH! on my lips.

"But of course it was you! Clever girl!" He pulls a face. "You even made the Other Dress look..." he struggles to find a kind adjective before spitting out "...*relevant.*"

At this point he doesn't need to know I'm the one who suggested the wearing of the Other Dress... and at risk of being accused of racial stereotyping... Jimmy is best described as Fat Buddha.

Short, plump and balding. He's wearing an open vintage Hawaiian shirt that proudly shows off his three chest hairs.

I'm in the process of deflecting his praise (as I do...) when a frisson of excitement radiates from the inside bar and outwards across the entire rooftop.

The Cool People try to maintain their coolness, but most fail and start losing their shit to some degree. Just as I'm wondering

184

what the big fucking deal is, Simon stands up and waves at the doorway.

"Tom! Over here!"

And there he is.

The sexiest man alive.

Tomcat Hardy.

Lead singer of supergroup Seven - and apparently Simon's new BFF.

Why am I not surprised...?

Walking over - smiling a little self-consciously - towards us.

And in reality? Hotter than all freaking hell.

Tall, lean muscles... long, golden brown curls... golden brown skin... a vintage Zeppelin t-shirt (minus the sleeves) that's been worn threadbare, well-loved black jeans, a beaten-up straw Panama and black rubber thongs.

"Fuck me dead!' Eloise mutters under her breath.

"Dying." I whisper back. "Literally. Dying."

As I temporarily lose the ability to form thought processes and perform basic motor skills, my phone slips right out of my hand...

and slides right under the daybed. I drop to my hands and knees trying to locate it when I hear...

"Where'd she go...? She was right here... *What the fuck are you doing down there???*"

And if, like Alice, I could find a rabbit hole under this piece of furniture to fall down, that'd be kinda great. Because right now, the Sexiest Man Alive is right behind me... and I am head down, bum up under a couch.

And just when it couldn't possibly get worse, I have a flashback to Simon hacking inches off the bottom of this skirt... and I have a terrible feeling that while I don't know exactly how much the Sexiest Man Alive can see right now, I'm pretty sure it's not my best angle.

Kill. Me. Now.

After what seems like forever, my fingertips hit hard, smooth phone case. I fish it out, extract my upper body and turn to see Simon... and The Sexiest Man Alive trying very hard not to smile.

"Lost my phone..." I mutter superfluously.

Babe! Is that seriously the best you can do...???

Simon offers me a hand to help me up.

"Sid, this is Tom. Tom, this is my bestie Cressida."

"Hey *Cress*ida..." he says my name thoughtfully. "You weren't there last night..."

It's a statement, not a question.

His voice is soft, rich and husky. If I didn't already know he's from North Carolina, the slight hint of a residual Southern drawl would give the game away.

"Mmmmm." I nod... so now I have apparently lost the power of speech...

Shit! Did he just say he noticed I wasn't there...?

"The guy who owns this place got married yesterday - she did the flowers. She's ridiculously talented. It was bigger than Texas..."

God bless Simon for trying to help me out.

"This place rocks!" he enthuses. "Fucking loving the artwork - it'd be kick-ass on an album cover..."

"The guy who does them is here somewhere... oh... over there!"

Ah! There you go!

Talking like an almost normal person.

Great job, you!

I spot Diego and point him out in the crowd.

"I can introduce you if you like... He's asked me to model for his next one..."

"Oh my fucking God! Shut up!!! You said yes, right...? You have such great tits." Simon is impressed.

"Didn't say yes... didn't say no...?"

Tom - after glancing down to verify Simon's assessment of my assets - raises a quizzical eyebrow.

"Which position...?" he asks. Quietly.

"I think he said The Trapeze...?"

It vaguely registers that I should Google *Karma Sutra* and *trapeze* before committing. And then I have a little freak out, because I am somehow discussing the Karma Sutra with the sexiest man alive... and he seems disarmingly well-versed on the subject.

Lowering my gaze to avoid his, I notice the holes in that well-loved t-shirt reveal glimpses of belly. Golden brown skin and a little sprinkle of hair. Hmmmm... Sexy much!

"Who gets to hold you?"

His lips hold the faintest suggestion of a smile.

"Oh..."

My mouth falls open. Hadn't thought of that... was so preoccupied with the no top part, I completely forgot about the Other Bits...

"I didn't ask..."

At which point we're interrupted by a pack of loud, confident, predatory girls.

"Hi Tom! I'm Riley - can we get some selfies...?"

Riley has spent much time and effort trying to look carelessly thrown together, from her very long, tousled silver Mermaid-waved hair to her expert I-wake-up-like-this make up.

"Sure."

He smiles - but not enthusiastically - as he allows himself to be lead away from me and Simon. Well played, Mermaid Girl.

With that glorious distraction removed, I become aware that through the very pleasant and rapidly escalating Mojito-induced fuzziness, there's stuff knocking in the back of my brain.

The girl on the boat...

Involuntarily I shudder. A little tremor of guilt for abandoning her... which I quell by draining my glass. Can't help but hope if I keep sinking these lime'n'rum bliss bombs I'll be too drunk to dream at all...

Hang on... there's something else...

"Oh... *Baby!!!*" I exclaim, checking my phone for an update. And...

Nothing.

"Forfuckssake! How long does it take to push out a baby...?"

I do a quick scan of our crew... gay men, party girls, playboys... nope. Nobody here will be any help at all. *Hmmphf!* Should have asked the Doctor, shouldn't you...?

The Selfie Precedent set, Tom becomes the trophy in a game of Keepings Off by the more socially ambitious groups on the roof and he keeps getting swept seemingly further and further away from us. Which is sort of a relief that I can just relax and enjoy myself... instead of feeling freaked out and inadequate that I can't form intelligent (let alone engaging...) sentences around him.

The shadows lengthen and the light softens as the sun slides down towards the horizon. Clouds have been slowly but surely building. The sky is now quite violet, the air thick and heavy with the anticipation of a storm.

And fuelled by a steady consumption of Mojitos and the odd samosa, I set about being a sociable kinda Birthday Girl...

I talk yoga classes with Eloise the Creative Accountant. She religiously does Iyengar. I half-heartedly do Hatha. We are, however, in agreement that Hot Yoga is a really bad and disgusting idea...

I talk fashion with Jimmy Quan, who's very passionate about Golden Years of Hollywood glamour and the womanly curves that went with it. I tell him how much I love him for not expecting a woman to have the body of a twelve-year old boy...

I let Dave the photographer flirt with me. That Dave is not particularly tall, kinda chunky and has messy, spiky hair, always makes me think of Sonic Hedgehog.

And I talk absolutely anything and everything with the highly fascinating fashion assistant, Indigo.

Possibly the most interesting person on this whole rooftop - pale, refined Elven features... platinum blond pixie-cropped hair... quick witted and keenly observant... and looking seriously amazing in a vintage Gucci silk scarf that she's twisted into a halter top and cut-off jeans. Boys and girls find her equally fascinating, and she indicates no preference for either.

Every increasingly inebriated conversation is punctuated regularly with me checking my phone for a baby update.

Every time a disappointing Nada.

This is starting to drive me nuts.

Then I have a terrible thought - what if everything isn't okay...?

I tell Indi I have to go to the loo, and go off in search of somewhere quiet to call TBJ.

Fortunately there's nobody kissing in the little dead-end corner just past the mens room (as is usually the case...)

I ask Siri to call TBJ and it goes straight to voicemail.

Instantly I think that her phone is off because something's wrong and she's at the hospital.

(ME) Hey any baby news???

The little blip starts bouncing immediately.

To look at TBJ, you'd expect her to text capitalised and punctuated essays with one index finger, squinting. However the TBJ anomaly is that she's innately *techy*. She's an early adopter, unsentimental adapter and a crazy-fast learner.

(TBJ) Still waiting

Talking about inducing

(ME) Yuck

(TBJ) Should have gone the C-section

No mess no fuss

(ME) Where ru?

(TBJ) Football

post game social

And bang! bang! bang! She's letting fly with a barrage of hilarious texts that I have no hope of keeping up with, criticising everything from the boring speeches, to the bad facelifts, to the unsexy baggy shorts the players are wearing... She's clearly very bored and I clearly have very Mojito-impaired motor skills... which makes for a very one-sided conversation. I hear a male voice say something, and I think it's directed at me.

"Huh?" It comes out distracted... as I look up from my phone, giggling at the thought of my triggered, bored, judgey and opinionated mother... and straight into the amber eyes of Tomcat Hardy. "Hang on a minute... " as my eyes go back to the bouncing blip.

And Tomcat is frowning - both confused and bemused - because I'm guessing Mr Rockstar isn't in the habit of having to wait for attention.

"I said, if I was him I'd be here."

He's taking a sip from a beer bottle as he hands me a Mojito. This is so goddam weird, there can only be one logical explanation... I'm so drunk I'm imagining things. So I reach up and pinch his arm.

"Youch! What the...?"

Hmmmm... so it's not the Mojitos talking... Good to know...

"Sorry! Just checking you're not a figment of my hyperactive imagination... You were saying...?"

Could this be any weirder...? No. It could not.

"Your boyfriend. You've been checking your phone like every fucking five seconds."

"Oh... no-no-no... no... it's not... I don't..."

194

Hmmm... the Cohesive Sentence is proving challenging.

Let's try that again...

Deep breath...

"I don't have a boyfriend. My sister is having a baby... but that should be a song... If I Was Him I'd Be Here..."

"Now how is that even possible ...?"

"Having a baby...???"

Surely he spends enough time practicing.

"You not having a boyfriend."

He's shaking his head and starting to laugh.

"Oh very easily. I'm pretty bad at it." I laugh. "You should ask Simon - he has several theories."

"I will be asking him..." he says with a sly smile. "And yeah. It fucking should be... Hey! Happy Birthday!"

He clinks his beer bottle against my cocktail glass.

Omg! Suddenly I remember...

I *do* have something kinda intelligent to say to him.

Why didn't I think of this before -

"Hey!" I say possibly a bit too loudly. "You know my best friend Sabine."

He looks at me blankly. As people often do. For some reason they find it difficult to commit those two seemingly very simple syllables to memory.

"Small loud blonde girl. She played on your last album."

"Ah! Sexy Cello Girl!" he grins. "She had a thing with our bass player, Matt..."

"Mmmmm... I heard."

Nodding knowingly. I raise an eyebrow.

"It was a hot thing..."

"It was a crazy hot thing. She messed with him. Big time. What is it with you damn Melbourne girls...?"

He raises his beer to his lips, then pauses.

"I thought you'd left me without saying goodbye."

"Oh no." I shake my head theatrically. " I can't leave without Simon. He has the *keys!*"

I pat my hands over my body to demonstrate my predicament, then shrug.

"No pockets. See...?"

His eyes follow my hands, but he seems to be missing my point about the pockets.

"So you would actually leave me without saying goodbye..."

196

Mock serious. Teasing me.

"Surely you had enough flirty little things fighting over you out there to make you happy, Mister Rockstar...?"

"You know what *would* make me happy?" he asks quietly, frowning.

And suddenly he's quite serious.

"Sitting on a sofa with a pretty girl... drinking beer, eating pizza and watching tv. Wondering if I should try to kiss her... Like a regular guy... I'm up to my two hundred and eightieth fucking day living like a hothouse flower in a hotel room. I'd kill for some kind of normal."

"*Try* to kiss her??? Like anybody would say no to you..." I scoff at him.

(And this is most definitely the Mojitos talking...)

"Would you...?"

He moves quite close to me.

"Would I what...?"

Is it just me, or is he very confusing?

(Or is this the Mojito's comprehension skills talking...?)

"Would you say no...?" He sounds somewhat serious, a bit amused and a tiny bit puzzled. He can't work out if I'm playing games or if I really am completely clueless.

It's the latter, Honey...

"Oh I'm all about beer'n'pizza!"

"I'm talking kissing. Would you say no...?"

I frown, giving it very serious consideration.

"No-oo...'

It comes out softly, slowly and deliberately.

"Is that no... or no... you wouldn't... say no..." Suddenly he shakes his head and laughs out loud. "Shit! Now you've got me talking in riddles..."

Not aware that I was talking in riddles, Mister Rockstar... but anyway...

"If we were sitting on my blue velvet couch... hmmmm... Yes!... I think I would probably let you kiss me."

"And what about now...?"

"What about now???"

I once again have no freaking idea what we're talking about.

"Me. Trying to kiss you. Right here. Right now."

"Oh... think I'd need to think about that..."

He shakes his head, laughing at me and is about to say something when his back pocket buzzes. He sighs as he checks it, like he's confirming his worst suspicions.

"Fuck, my car is here - I gotta bail. I wanna stay..."

"Oh yeah! It's going to be wild when that storm hits..."

He shakes his head at me, looking completely bemused.

"I've never met anyone like you before..."

And I just kinda frown at him because... really... what are you supposed to say to that...? (Oh! I bet Mermaid Girl would know...)

"So... have you thought about it?" he asks quite softly.

"About what???" I whisper back theatrically... because apparently we are now Talking Softly...

"If you'd let me kiss you..."

"Hmmmm..."

I frown for a second, then tap a finger on my cheek.

"You may kiss me right here."

"Not here...?" as he reaches up very slowly and rests a finger softly on my lips.

"Nope." I shake my head emphatically, then tap my cheek decisively. "Right here, Mister Rockstar... on one condition..."

He smiles ruefully and raises a quizzical eyebrow.

"What...?"

"I want a selfie with Mister Rockstar!"

"Seriously...?"

He shakes his head, laughing, and takes my phone out of my hand.

"If I ever get you on that blue velvet couch, your ass is mine."

And I nod.

Because that sounds quite reasonable.

"Fair enough."

And I watch him turn and walk away, still shaking his head.

And I completely forgot any of this happened... until days later... when flicking through my photos I come across a burst of selfies...

Undeniably me...

Having my cheek kissed and my ear whispered into...

By undeniably the Sexiest Man in the World.

Sunday 11:53pm
Only when I sleep...

Massive droplets of rain pelt us as we run from the car to the stairs. Like most things that happen with little planning and no expectation - from start to finish - it was the best. As afternoon slid into evening and the thunder clouds rolled in, summer finally conceded to autumn right before us. It's like the whole city knew that this was to be the last day of running around half-naked for a very long time and everyone was out for a last hurrah.

Feeling strangely empowered from Dr Wolfe's house call - and liquored up on a significant number of cocktails - I was in pretty good form. The liberating satisfaction of just rolling with it... not trying to *be* anything or make anything happen... just being in the moment and having an absolute hoot so doing.

"Shhhhh!"

"No - you shhhhh!!!"

"You & Danh are in lu-u-u-urve!"

"You blew off Tomcat Hardy! I cannot believe you blew off Tomcat Hardy...! What are you like???"

Simon and I are like a pair of five-year olds teetering precariously up the stairs, more than a little inebriated.

Miraculously I remember to transfer most of my laundry to the dryer (yay me!) then pull on Josh Gillespie's Nirvana t-shirt before sliding drunk and exhausted into bed.

He is sitting in the front row of a home theatre.

He's wearing jeans and an open neck pale blue shirt.

Three other men are seated neither close nor far away.

Wolfgang leads her in.

They all wear jeans and t-shirts, like regular guys at the movies. She wears very short sky blue shorts and a white Lacoste polo.

Her terrified eyes take it all in - the cinema chairs, the men.

So many men.

Her breath shudders.

She's trying hard not to panic, but she can't see a way out. She's trying not to think about what they're going to do to her, but she can't help but fear it will be worse than anything she can possibly imagine.

Oh God no! No!

Wolfgang seats her next to Him, then takes a seat directly behind her.

"Good evening, my dear. Sorry we are late getting started, but there was far too much activity outside. Thank heaven for this storm..."

He turns his whole body to face her, leaning in very close.

"We didn't get off to the best of starts now, did we...?"

He raises a hand to touch the shiny, bluish-purple bruise on her temple. She closes her eyes and prays once again that this is a nightmare and she'll wake up.

"See what you made me do? Let's not be... foolish... again. Yes...? So..."

He turns back to the screen.

"Tonight we are going to watch a movie. I'm a bit of an amateur cinematographer. I have a particular fondness for editing... cutting things together. Are you familiar with the work of Sergei Eisenstein...? Battleship Potemkin??? Ah... never mind... I think we can start now please, Wolfgang."

Her eyes dart around the room uncertainly as the lights fade.

A movie. How bad can a movie be? ... Why are there five men? ... Could she beat them to the door?... What are they going to do to her...???

A picture appears on the screen. It's the same room as last night - bed, sofa, table for two, room service cart.

Same flowers... Fantin Latour roses... lime hellebores...

It is also him, but he is a much younger man. However he wears the same clothes.

"So my dear... This is 1982... and the room is familiar, yes...?" He turns and she flinches, feeling his breath on her face.

"This is the actual room at that very famous Paris hotel. You recognise it, yes...? Maybe not... And this is me as a younger man. A young man with no focus, my father used to say. He was most concerned that nothing interested me... I had no *passion*... Not studies or work... or even women. For some reason, he was especially concerned about my lack of interest in women. So he sent me to Paris for an 'initiation', he called it..."

We see him go to the door, and a beautifully groomed young blonde wearing a chartreuse silk shift dress enters.

They make barely audible small talk in French.

204

His running commentary continues over the top it.

He offers her Champagne and they sit at the table.

She is trying to be charming, but he is giving her no encouragement. He is bored.

"So we can see she is trying so hard - and her work ethic is admirable, is it not? - but I really have no interest in her at all."

She stands and walks gracefully around the table. Standing behind him, she smiles and gently caresses his neck.

"Ah God... here we go..."

Bored. Sarcastic.

Her manicured hand slides over his shirt towards the waistband of his pants. She undoes his belt.

"She has clearly had much practise at doing *that*..."

The men snigger.

Our girl shudders.

Deftly she undoes the button and reaches down to unzip him.

He sighs in boredom.

"So... I am sitting there wondering how do I make this stop... because I really just want her to stop... And then it occurs to me that I want to hurt her. I want very badly to hurt her..."

His fingers close like a vice over her wrist and squeeze hard. Too hard.

Suddenly she realises there is something very, very wrong.

She cries out in pain.

She breaks free and bolts for the door.

"And suddenly this becomes interesting to me!" he laughs.

He chases after her and grabbing a handful of her pretty hair, yanks it as hard as he can. She screams, stumbling backwards. Now she is panicking.

No! Make it stop!

The more she struggles, the more excited he becomes. And the more force he exerts.

"And just like that... my interest in women is... aroused..." he laughs. He turns to his new victim. "Open your eyes, my dear!" he whispers in her ear. "It gets so much more exciting..."

The pretty escorte breaks away from him and tries again to make it to the door. She is screaming frantically for help. He tries to grab her hand, but only succeeds in catching her pinky finger. He reefs it sideways.

"I heard it snap..." he whispers in delight. "I heard it snap!"

Oh God! Help! Help her! Somebody help her...

She cries out in agony, terrified now. Screaming her lungs out for help. She reaches out, frantically clutching for the door handle. He lunges from behind, clamping his hand over her mouth.

"Oh shut up, bitch! *Shut up!*"

She bites his hand. Hard.

"Oh you really shouldn't have done that..."

He tackles her, riding her into the oriental carpet, crashing hard on top of her. He rips up her dress and uses all of the brute force of his rage against her.

In the dark cinema, our poor girl's chest is shuddering as she shrinks into the theatre chair, crying silently without tears.

On the screen, he needs to make the screaming stop. He wraps his hands around her throat and chokes her until he squeezes the last breath of life out of her.

There is a lap dissolve into the same hotel room, but he's opening the door to a redhead.

"So... this is how my game started... of course it's never quite as exciting as the first time..."

It cuts to a different girl... then another... then another... all in the same dress. Then it cuts to different expensive hotel rooms, but still the same dress.

208

Our girl shrinks into the theatre seat, sobbing uncontrollably.

How many girls? How many girls...???

Over and over.

It always ends the same way.

Over and over and over.

The screaming getting louder and louder and louder.

Make it stop. Oh God. Please! Make it stop!

In the cinema, He turns to face her. He reaches out to slide his fingers through her hair. Grabbing a handful, he pulls it. Hard.

"The door is right over there..." he whispers into her ear, his lips so close she can feel the anticipation in his breath. "Run! Go on... Run!"

And she sinks her teeth into his forearm as hard as she can. She attacks his face like an animal, trying to gouge his eyes.

Wolfgang springs out of his seat and hauls her off him. He punches her hard in the face.

She crumples to the ground.

She pretends to be unconscious.

He is so wild with rage he has gone very, very quiet. Someone hits the lights. They all stand over her body, avoiding each other's gaze.

"It's not late - would you like a new girl...? It won't prove difficult on a night like this - "

"*I'm bleeding!*" he roars. "Fucking bitch bit me like a dog!!! It's all wrong. All wrong. I want to leave here."

"Where do you want to go? Launceston is about two hundred nautical miles, Sydney is almost four... or New Zealand is eleven hundred."

"North."

"What do we do with this one...?"

Her pulse is thudding in her ears.

She can taste blood in her mouth from the gaping holes where two of her teeth have been knocked out. She keeps playing possum, parting her lips slightly so the blood pooling in her mouth can drain onto the carpet.

"*Feed her to the fucking sharks!* How can I play with her? She's a fucking animal."

After a pause that seems like eternity, Wolfgang speaks very softly.

"So why don't we treat her like one...? Make her your quarry."

He looks suddenly thoughtful and his eyes light up.

"What if we let her escape... and we hunt her all over the ship..."

His tongue darts over his lips like a reptile.

And he smiles with his mouth, but not his cruel, cold eyes.

"We wait til we're in open water - in case she gets to the decks..." He nods thoughtfully. Wondering if he has enough cameras. "Yes... yes..." he muses. "Now get her out of my sight."

Monday 3.05am

We really should stop meeting like this…

"Sid! Sid! CRESSIDA! Wake up!... Wake up!!!"

A voice.

Loud.

Getting louder.

Hands shaking me violently. Feeling like I'm being dragged from one world into another.

With a gasp I open my eyes.

Simon is crouched over my body. Panic-stricken.

There's a soft knock on the front door.

He gently places his hands on me.

"It's okay. You're okay."

But his eyes are frightened and wary.

"I'll be back in a second."

I close my eyes and try to breathe.

In... Out...

In... Out...

My face is soaked with tears. My pulse is still thudding in my throat. Involuntarily my head starts shaking and all I can say is No.

Softly.

Over and over and over again.

No.

"She was screaming... crying... I tried to wake her for nearly an hour... I thought you needed a fucking shaman and drugs to dream like that..."

I open my eyes slowly and there are blue ones - every colour of the ocean - looking back into mine. I glance up at the window over my bed. It's dark outside.

"What time is it?" My voice is a husky croak. My throat is killing me.

"A bit after three."

Mick's voice is soft and he looks concerned.

"You okay...? Simon, could you get her some water please, Mate...?"

I realise I'm shaking all over and I can't stop hearing their screams and I can't stop seeing the green dress crash tackled to the carpet.

Over and over.

"Can you sit up...?" He gently pulls me upright, placing the pillow behind my back. I'm freezing cold now... and shaking so hard I'm nearly convulsing.

Mick takes the glass from Simon and holds it carefully at my lips, gently tilting it so I can take a sip. Then placing it on the bedside table, he gently sits down on the bed.

"Hey!" he says so softly, carefully taking my hands in his and squeezing gently but firmly. "It's okay. It's just a dream. You're okay."

His hands feel strong, capable and reassuring. I look right into his almost handsome face and wish he'd wrap his arms around me so I could collapse into his soft, grey sweater.

But he doesn't, so I sit there and shake my head.

No. No it's not just a dream and it's not okay.

I've seen what he does. He's a monster.

We could not be any fucking further from okay.

I put my hands over my eyes, like I can somehow make it go away. He asks almost hesitantly.

"Can you tell me what you saw...?"

He feels me shudder and I shake my head.

I don't think I can, but I know I have to.

I have a terrible feeling that I'm the only hope she has...

Hands still over my eyes, I take a deep breath and hit rewind in my head. Gently he places a hand on my knee, giving it a fatherly, reassuring squeeze.

"I know you can do it. Come on... Just say the first thing that comes into your head..."

Open water... nautical miles... home theatre.

How voices sound in the cool-room at work...

Suddenly I sit up straight, both hands over my mouth.

"*She's on a boat!* They've got her on a boat!"

Mick's eyes search my face.

"What kind of boat?"

"A big one. Like a super yacht. I've done flowers on them before." And suddenly it all makes sense.

"There's usually a media room on the lowest deck... her cell is a cool-room... The marina is not even ten minutes from where they grabbed her..."

He pulls out his phone.

"Hey! We need the MTPC applications for every vessel currently berthed at the Melbourne Marina... Now! Specifically flag codes from foreign vessels. Get Andy out of bed and tell him I'll meet him at hq in about thirty... There has to be a ransom demand coming soon..."

He ends the call, turning his attention back to me.

"*It's not political! Why won't you listen to me?!*" For fuck's sake! Why can't he see he's got it wrong...? "*He's a fucking serial killer!!!* You need to search every boat. Now! They're going to weigh anchor soon... She's running out of time!"

"You know how the law works. We can't just go in and turn stuff upside down - especially with the kind of people who own big boats. We need a warrant... and we need reasonable grounds to get one. I think we're onto something... but we're not there yet... Hey! - where'd *Serial Killer* come from??? You need to tell me everything."

He rubs his hands up and down my arms. Trying to get me focussed.

"Start at the beginning. Take it slowly."

He gives me a reassuring smile.

"I'm recording now, okay...?"

I take a deep shuddering breath.

"It's okay. You can do it."

I don't know if I can, but I know I have to.

I tell him every hideous detail. By the time I reach her pretending to be unconscious on the ground again, I am numb with the horror of it all.

He presses stop on his phone. When I finally open my eyes, wiping the tears away roughly with the back of my hands, he's frowning. Thoughtfully.

"What if... we *have* got this all wrong... What if there's no ransom demand...?"

My reply comes out too loud and almost hysterical.

"You *have* got it wrong! There's *no demand* coming. And she's going to die tonight. And I'm going to have to watch it *if you don't find her!!!*"

218

Simon appears with coffee mugs and a plate of sourdough toast with lots of butter, strategically dotted with Vegemite.

"Here! Eat! Vegemite makes everything better..."

"Cheers Mate!"

Mick seems grateful for the interruption, grabs a piece and takes a man-size bite. I notice he has beautiful teeth.

I pick up a piece and stare warily at it, then I gingerly take a bite. Warm, crunchy, melty-buttery, immensely umami salty - it's strangely comforting and does make me feel a little better.

"That's some gift you've got there."

"How is this a fucking gift??"

The words come out very quietly - but still faintly hysterical.

"Seeing lottery numbers would be a gift... seeing a cure for cancer would be a gift... Tom Hardy naked in the shower would be a gift..."

Oh shit!

That wasn't supposed to come out.

Simon splutters a mouthful of coffee. Suddenly I find my piece of toast extremely interesting. I realise I'm going to have to make eye contact sooner or later.

I take a deep breath and look up at him. He's shaking his head and the corners of his mouth are fighting to curl up into a smile. Can't help but notice that he's so much more attractive without his game face on.

"Too much information, Rich Girl."

Then he snaps back into work mode, barking orders into his phone. Ending the call, he takes a long, hard look at me.

"Are you okay...?"

I nod vaguely.

"No you're not. Take it easy, hey...? Is there anything else you remember...?"

I shake my head equally vaguely. Exhausted. Sickened. Full of dread.

"Nope. Just find her. *Please!* You have to..."

He asks if he can send me photos to id, should any suspects turn up. I'm not crazy about the idea, because that would mean this sicko is real, and I'm kind of clinging to the remote possibility that it's all just my imagination...

I take a deep breath and nod.

I'll burn that bridge
when I come to it...

By the time Simon bundles me into the car to drive me to work a couple of hours later, I feel like I've been awake forever.

Winter has arrived - and with a vengeance.

Grey, raining and bitterly cold.

Melbourne Weather.

And it's a bad day to feel like Dead Woman Walking.

Mondays are always full on. I'll be out for most of the day looking after corporate clients - refurbishing or replacing huge and elaborate arrangements in hotels and offices. I need to be pretty portable. I'm wearing tight, stretchy olive cargo pants so I have plenty of pockets, my new black cashmere turtleneck and chestnut RM Williams ankle boots. Simon frowned... then added a purple and lime wool scarf (which if you look really closely, you'll notice the 'pretty' pattern is actually skulls) before nodding and pronouncing *Better!*

"Hey! You do the flowers at the Palace today, don't you? We're nearly out of coffee - do you have time to duck into Mama Java and get some Dark Side?"

Here in Melbourne, we have two religions - football and coffee. When I say we take our coffee seriously, we are not merely talking necessary caffeine in a bag. We are talking specialty roasting companies that treat coffee with the same respect and sophistication as wine. One does not simply *buy coffee* - we want to know what it is, where it came from, the name of the person's dog who grew it and whether its going to taste like almonds, dark chocolate, raw sugar or nectarines. Mama Java has a store in the hotel's posh and expensive retail plaza. I nod a vague *yes.*

I wish I could stop thinking about the girl...

But I can't.

The workroom is a whole different world from when we were last here. The excitement, novelty and drama that always comes with a huge job has reverted to the mundane and very workmanlike Business As Usual. Bare, tanned limbs are rugged up. Smiling, expectant faces have been replaced with slightly grim *here we fucking go again* expressions. There's no time for small talk or weekend catch up as we hit the ground running. That'll have to wait til after the last courier pick up at 3pm...

If you know anything about flowers, you'll know artificial heat is not their friend. So... our shop and workroom has no heating... Nada! ...which means for the next six months, it's going to feel like we work in a fucking mausoleum. I feel especially sorry for the junior minions who have to unpack the flowers stored over the weekend in the cool-room, going from cold into even colder and having to empty the freezing water from every freezing glass vase to change it.

I hear a voice echo from the cool-room (*"Can someone tell me if all these white freesias are still sold???"*) and I have a flashback to my first dream.

Involuntarily I shudder, then decide keeping busy - very busy! - is my best bet to stop this whole dream thing doing my head in. I grab a vase of spectacular and delicate pink parrot tulips from the work bench and take it out to the shop while I wait for my next order..

"Psssssssssssst!"

A soft, low, theatrical whisper as I walk past the elegant, gilt writing desk. Slumped languidly in the matching gilt chair - which seems improbably petite and delicate - is the powerful, panther like form of Sebastian Marchesi. One elbow rests casually on the desk, hand suspended lazily in the air with an addressed gift card and a bunch of hundred dollar bills resting casually between his index and middle fingers. Like he does every Monday morning...

He is ridiculously handsome - in an Older Man kind of way. Though his dark hair is greying at the temples, his dark, dark brown eyes often have the glint of a naughty school boy. Immaculately groomed and tastefully, understatedly expensive. He is also ridiculously wealthy, starting with nightclubs as a young buck and progressing to more sophisticated ventures like hotels, hedge funds and real estate. There are sometimes whispers about dirty dealings, but he's far too clever and meticulous to ever get himself implicated - and it would be my father's job to keep him out of jail if he ever did - which is, I guess, why he trusts me to do this for him.

What exactly...? You're about to find out...

"Hmmmm... they look perfect. In that vase. Just like that. On the hall table."

With a wink, he hands me the card (addressed, as usual, to Holly Golightly) and the cash, then stands smoothly and saunters out the door.

224

"Kitty...? Kitty Cat!"

Troy is screaming impatiently as he somewhat frantically scans the workroom.

"Get into the Palace right now! I've just had Harold on the phone - all the lilies in the atrium are stone motherless dead. He's having a fucking cow..."

"That all only went in on Friday, but they would have had the air con cranked up all weekend..."

Helpful Hint #2 - cut flowers also do not like artificial cooling.

"I don't want the how's and why's... I want it fixed. *Now!*"

"Leaving as we speak..." as I ring up the $500 on the cash register and stuff the notes in the drawer. "Just gotta drop something off for Seb Marchesi on the way through..."

Troy nods a curt *okay*. There are a few names you can drop that Troy will stop the world turning for... Marchesi is one of them.

Van keys clenched in my teeth, I grab a huge bucket of orange tiger lilies on my way out, only just delivered and still wrapped in cellophane, and with the vase of parrot tulips still sitting on my other hip like a toddler, I make my way out to a work van to start getting shit done. With all the weight bearing I do, it's seriously unfair that I'm not fitter...

Still feeling a bit shaky but a little more human, I drive a couple of blocks, then turn into the service entrance of Marquis. This beautiful twenty storey monument to stealth wealth is the baby of Seb Marchesi. If Stratus is very New York, Marquis is Paris. High tech security has number plate recognition and it's familiar with all the Le Jardin vans. Like I said, you could seriously break into anywhere in a Le Jardin van and nobody would bat an eyelid...

There's a very private elevator in a discreet corner. I punch a six digit code into the keypad and the doors glide silently open. The interior is completely mirrored and I try very hard not to catch my reflection. A hangover on top of a freaky dream episode is not pretty.

The elevator has only one stop - the penthouse.

With a discreet *ding!* the doors open onto a plush, yet understated foyer. Polished antique parquet floor... huge black and white abstract lithographs... hand-carved front door stained so dark it's

226

nearly black adorned with a medieval brass lion door knocker. I key in another six digit code, and it swings open.

And just like I've done every Monday for the past year or so, I walk in and carefully place the vase on the long, elegant console table in front of me and drop the card into the exquisite porcelain trinket tray, which is hand-painted with a winged horse. Sometimes there's also a fancy gift box... pale blue from Tiffany's... orange from Hermes... red from Cartier...

Yes.

Somebody is a very spoilt girl. However I have no idea who *Somebody* is... other than it's not Sebastian Marchesi's wife and it's a pretty safe bet that Holly Golightly is not her real name.

I was sworn to secrecy. Nobody knows I deliver here - oh, except Simon, but he doesn't count... He often asks if I've snooped around the apartment to find something to identify our Mystery Mistress, but I have not. I was directed to place the weekly offering on the hall table and leave. Seb trusts me, and I won't abuse that trust. And if the mention of *trust* makes you think of his 'poor' wife, don't be sorry for her... Despite being supermodel attractive, Bo Marchesi is one of the most un-beautiful people God ever put breath into. We call her The Boa Constrictor. If you're lucky, you'll never meet her - but sadly I can't make any promises...

When it comes to Private Lives of the Rich and Famous, there's not much the florist doesn't know. Because people with pretty manners (not to mention the Upwardly Mobile, desperately clambering for Acceptance...) always send flowers. From pre-birth to death (and every birthday, illness, relationship, affair, promotion and faux pas in between), we find out pretty much first. And we never tell! To the outside world Sebastian and Bo Marchesi are the perfect couple living a dream life. Happy. Handsome. Successful. Two beautiful children (one of each, naturally)... Rumours of political ambitions... possibly a seat in Parliament with a view to Prime Minister (and he'd make a very photogenic leader...)

But like a lot of relationships, the reality comes without the beauty filters of social media...

And this is why he needs to know his secret is safe with me. So I give Miss Golightly's tulips one last zhuzh, pull a cloth from my back pocket to carefully wipe the table top in case I've missed any rogue drops of water, and head on in to the Palace to stop Harold the hysterical Head of Housekeeping from spinning off his tits.

Once the Tiger Lily Crisis in the atrium is resolved and all my mess disposed of, I head up to Mama Java.

Foot traffic is pretty light in the plaza at this hour of the morning. I grab my bag of Dark Side beans and try to work out the plan of attack for the rest of my day. A man passes me as I leave the store. I only glance at his face, but it sends a jolt of electricity to my heart.

My skin prickles and my pulse starts thudding so loudly in my ears I'm scared he can hear it. I'm also scared that for the split-second I looked into his pale, almost colourless eyes he saw the recognition, then terror, in mine.

I fumble with my phone and text Mick.

He's here!!!

He's here right now!

Palace... Mama Java...

Sending photo

Instantly he replies.

"Do not do that!

Cameras everywhere in Palace

Getting id now"

I wouldn't call myself a brave person, so I don't know where I found the courage to flick my camera onto video and - pretending to make a FaceTime call - hold it up to film him walk right towards me as he leaves the shop. With shaking hands I send it to Mick.

Instantly my phone rings.

"Stop it right now! We have it under control."

But what if they don't...?

"He's just gone out the exit next to Dolce Vita... he's on the promenade heading towards the marina."

My teeth chatter as I follow him outside onto the wide walkway that runs along the Yarra River. The wind is strong and icy, belting in right off the bay.

"Tell me you're not following him...? Stop it! He's dangerous. *Stand down immediately!*"

But my legs can't stop walking and the only thought in my head is I must not let him get away.

It's the only way to make it stop.

To make the hideous dreams stop.

An historic, three-mast cargo ship comes into view.

"He's just passing the Pollywoodside now..."

"Fucking hell Cressida! *Leave it alone!* Turn around and walk away. *Now!*"

"I don't think I can do that..."

I hang up on him and with shivering hands I flick my phone onto silent.

We walk for fifteen minutes, heading right into buffeting, icy wind. The whole way my eyes are streaming, my nose is dripping and my arms are tightly bundled across my chest.

Apart from the odd very committed jogger, a student on a bike and a passing female executive with the wind in her back, literally blowing her into work, peak hour is over and the river-front promenade is deserted. One solitary raven tries to land on a street light but gets blown off course. Embarrassed, his chunky little body comes to rest on an awning instead. He ruffles his shiny, black feathers, hoping nobody noticed.

I drop back a little and hope that if our psychopath chances to turn around he'll think I'm just a girl from one of the hundreds of Docklands apartments who ran out of coffee, like him.

Finally the Marina comes into view.

Neat lines of yachts and small boats are moored on the jetties that criss cross the river. He passes the little boats and heads towards a private jetty, where a massive boat with a gleaming black hull and grey superstructure is moored.

Her name is the Anenome.

I flinch, realising it's not a reference to the chirpy yet unremarkable floral namesake, but the marine predator who waves his venomous tentacles in the current to snare prey.

My heart sinks. There's a steel mesh security gate and fence.

He's going to get away from me.

He taps in the security code and disappears onto the boat.

I huddle in front of the huge frosted glass windows of the Marina offices, trying to look inconspicuous as I dial Mick.

"He's just boarded the Anenome." I whisper.

"*Get the fuck out of there right now!* I mean it! I will have you arrested."

He's roaring at me.

I hang up on him but pretend I'm still having a pleasant conversation - should anyone be watching me - and take the opportunity to look around. There isn't a soul in sight.

Some ravens are perched grimly on the security fence. My mind whirring, I absently count them.

Thirteen.

Frowning, I Google the Counting Crows rhyme.

And instantly wish I hadn't.

THIRTEEN beware of the devil himself...

But we already knew that, didn't we...?

Where the hell are the police...? What if they sail now...?

They're going to get away.

And all I can do is stand here and watch it happen...

Three of the men appear on deck.

They disembark and head to the security gate, picking up the two shopping trollies that have been left there on the way through. There's some swearing and head shaking at the security gate... *and one of them bends down and wedges the door open!* Talking amongst themselves, they wheel the trollies off the jetty and disappear behind some buildings. There's a carpark and a loading dock. I know the geography - we've done jobs here.

My pulse starts thudding even louder in my ears and my heart feels like it's going to explode. Like a woman possessed, my legs start propelling me towards the boat.

And I'm feeling my feet reverberate on the weathered timber planks as I walk out on the jetty - which feels like it's a mile long.

I slip through the open security gate.

I board the Anenome.

If I get caught, I'll hold up my coffee, play dumb, pretend to be lost and make like I thought this was my boat. I'm hoping the layout of this big boy's toy will be the same as the others I've been on.

From the outside, the main deck looks deserted.

I take the walkway along the port side and - yes! Thank you! - halfway along there's a door.

Unlocked.

Heart in my mouth, I open it... and I can see stairs to the lower deck.

With trembling knees and my heart thudding in my throat, I descend one flight, then another.

And I'm on the tank deck.

I pass a few closed doors. A chill goes up my spine and I somehow know that one is his cinema.

Opulent plush gives way to bare-bones and functional...

I know she must be close.

Two giant cool rooms.

One has a *Danger! Keep Out!* sign.

And three sliding bolts in addition to the latch.

My pulse is thudding and my fingers are trembling as I slide one... two... three...

I pull the latch and swing the door open - like I have hundreds of times before at work.

And I gasp. With astonishment. With relief.

There she is.

Startled. Wide-eyed. Bruised. Terrified.

But alive.

"It's okay." I quickly reassure her and carefully pull the door to, testing to see if it will slam shut. It doesn't. I grab the key from the hook next to the door, cross the tiny room and reach down to unlock the manacle from her wrist.

"Come on! Let's go!" I whisper urgently.

I've been so focussed on trying to free her, I've failed to notice her expression.

Fear. Suspicion. Hatred.

She shakes her head.

"No!"

What the actual fuck???

"Come on! We have to go! *Now!* "

I don't know how long I've been here, but it's already too long. How much time will it take three men to go out to the parking lot behind the buildings, load those two trollies with supplies, and come back...? Barely enough.

Barely enough!

Just two flights of stairs and she's free.

But she shakes her head. Almost petulantly.

"No. I know you're not saving me. I heard them last night..."

What the hell...? *Oh shit!*

"No - this isn't a game! I'm here to save y-"

I freeze. There are footsteps outside. There's nowhere to hide so all I can do is stare at the door. There's a few harsh, guttural words that I can only assume are obscenities, then the door is slammed and the bolts slide shut.

One. Two. Three.

And she only has to take in the look of horror on my face to know she was wrong.

And she bursts into tears.

I try not to panic. I also suppress the desire to yell *What the fuck is wrong with you?* at her.

Okay. Breathe. The police must be on the way.

And I repeat it out loud, to reassure myself as much as her.

"It's okay. The police are on the way."

"Are you a cop?"

"No. I'm a florist."

She - not surprisingly - looks very confused.

"I saw you in a dream."

From the look on her face, that doesn't make things any clearer.

"Are you okay? I saw him hit you... your teeth...?"

She nods, but she's looking at me sideways.

Like I'm a witch.

"And Bear is going to be okay."

That seals the deal. She gasps and almost smiles. And then she cries some more. She lets me unlock her wrist.

I search the room again.

Still nowhere to hide.

And no way out.

Phone!

Frantically I pull it out. My heart sinks. No signal.

Hopefully I pat the multiple pockets of my cargo pants, hoping for something to use as a weapon.

Keys... secateurs...

They'll only buy us a few minutes.

Okay.

They don't know I'm here and they don't know she's free. We have the element of surprise and she can fight like a goddam tiger. Maybe we could rush them and run for the stairs...

All the way to the stairs... all the way up the stairs... so, so far...

And what if they catch us...

Catch me...

And then my stomach convulses in horror as it dawns on me that I'm already caught.

And if the bad guys open the door first, there will be another girl in the green dress. With longish hair too dark to be blond and too fair to be brunette...

Was that a gunshot...?

Another.

And another.

We stare at each other, and I know she sees in my eyes exactly what I see in hers. The same question. Asking if we dare to hope...

Loud boots and yelling.

Getting closer and closer.

Til we can understand the words.

Police! Get down!... Clear!"

Systematically crashing doors open til they get to ours.

The voice is booming, harsh and terrifying.

She freezes on the bed. I sink to my knees.

The door is flung open and there is the biggest, fittest man I have ever seen in my life. Black jumpsuit, helmet and face mask. Armour, utility belt and weapon belts all over him.

"Chook to Phoenix. Two female hostages. No serious injuries to report. Tank deck is clear. I'm going to need another pair of hands, over."

He pulls down his mask and carefully crouches in front of her.

"You're okay."

His voice is surprisingly gentle.

"It's over. Let's get you out of here."

And he picks her up like a doll and carries her out of the room.

I've collapsed, slumped against the wall with relief.

Staring blankly straight ahead.

I hear a deep voice say softly *Going up!* as another Special Ops superhero bends down to scoop me up.

"I'm fine... I can walk. *Really!*... I'm a lot heavier than I look..."

And he just chuckles softly.

And I'm off the ground, in his ridiculously big arms.

Now I know right now my body is pumping more adrenaline and cortisol than it should reasonably be expected to handle... but

240

when I look up at my superhero I think he has the most beautiful eyes I've ever seen.

Brown. Kind. Twinkling.

With thick, dark lashes that are criminally long for a man.

He carries me through to the stairs. Someone calls out from the media room -

"Hey! Why does Tex always get the girl...?"

"Right place, right time, every time."

He laughs and I feel it in his chest, through his ceramic armour.

We get to the stairs.

"Seriously! I'm fine. You can't..."

"Can and will."

His eyes look like he's grinning under his mask.

"This is my kind of leg day."

And he carries me up those two almost vertical flights of stairs without missing a beat.

"Where am I putting this...?" he asks to no one in particular as we arrive at the stern of the main deck. Amongst the Special Ops guys in black, there's a small army of navy blue baseball caps and ballistic vests over regular clothes.

"Over here, Mate!"

A familiar voice calls out.

And he turns to see me.

And emotion spins through those ocean blue eyes like the wheel on a gameshow.

Surprise.

Confusion.

Concern.

Fear.

And... tick-tick-tick-tick... coming to rest on Anger.

My new superhero friend sets me carefully on my feet, holding me firmly upright for a few seconds.

"Just take it easy, yeah...? You might think you're okay, but shock can sneak up on you."

"Thank you." I try to say it, but I don't seem to have a voice. I feel like a three-year-old.

"You okay?" Mick asks. Tersely.

I nod. I vaguely notice Andy is next to him - with the same confusion and concern flashing through his eyes as he realises it's me. Mick clamps his hand around my wrist and mutters -

"I'll be back in a few minutes. I need to have a word with my asset."

And he drags me off the boat, along the jetty towards the carpark behind the Marina offices, away from the fray.

His fingers sink hard into my shoulders and he spins me to face him.

"*WHAT THE FUCK WERE YOU THINKING???*" he roars at me. His face contorted with anger. "How many times did I tell you to stop? That guy is dangerous. He's wanted in so many countries we could auction him for extradition... and you get yourself kidnapped by him!"

Ah... here's the thing...

He's *really* not going to like this...

"I wasn't kidnapped. They didn't know I was there. Technically I was... ahem!... a stowaway."

He stares at me. Long and hard.

And the wheel is spinning again.

Confusion. Disbelief. Anger.

Angrier. And Angrier. And Angrier.

Really. Angry.

He speaks so slowly and quietly it's almost a whisper.

"You...*voluntarily*... boarded that boat...?"

I nod slowly and swallow.

"Mmmmm..."

In retrospect, it was a pretty bad idea.

"What is wrong with you???"

And we're back to yelling...

"Do you have any idea how close you just came to getting yourself killed...?"

Actually, it's starting to dawn on me.

And Tex was right.

My knees are feeling weak and I'm fighting to stop my lower lip from trembling.

"It's my job to keep you safe. How can I fucking do that if you can't do as you're told?"

Losing the battle to control lower lip.

Lump building in throat.

"I just needed to... f-f-f-find her. To make it stop..."

Tears starting to sting in the corners of my eyes.

"Do you have any idea what it's like b-b-b-being haunted by shit like that and not knowing if it's real or if you're g-g-g-going -"

244

Shuddering gasp. A tear escapes and slides down my cheek.

"-*crazy*...? F-f-feeling like you're the only p-p-person who... who can make it stop...?"

"Oh no no no. Don't cry. Don't you dare fucking cry!"

And I dissolve into a flood of tears.

Of anger. Of fear. Of frustration.

And relief.

"Oh Jesus!"

Shaking his head with a sigh, he slides an arm around my shoulders and pulls me into his chest. And I sob pretty violently - although not remotely prettily, because I am not a Pretty Crier - into his ballistic vest.

"Please don't cry."

He gently raises my chin to look up at him and carefully wipes my tears away with his thumb.

"My Kryptonite. Pretty Girl Tears."

"Thank you."

My voice is thick with mucus and tears. I sniff loudly and wipe my nose with the back of my hand.

See? Not a Pretty Crier.

"I kinda need to get back to work..."

He laughs, with great irony.

"You're going nowhere. You have to be interviewed."

"But if I wasn't actually *kidnapped...* Can't we just pretend I was never there...?"

"No. No we cannot."

"But what do I say...?"

Starting to cringe. Because having to say how stupidly reckless I've just been out loud is going to be...

"You tell the truth. The whole truth. And I hope it's so awkward and embarrassing that you never put yourself in this situation again. Got it???"

And I did.

And it was awkward and embarrassing.

And if I am smart... I will never do anything like it again.

Officially, this is something that never happened - and this was made most clear to me in the interview room. Driving out of the Marina, there were fire trucks and police cordons everywhere. It was a 'toxic gas leak'.

They called work and told them I had been affected and had to go to hospital for observation. I handed over the keys and someone kindly returned the van to work for me.

Keeping the Wolfe from the door...

An unmarked car dropped me home and I hauled my exhausted and unprecedentedly relieved ass up the stairs.

And I am literally counting the steps until I'm in bed... and as my front door appears in view, so does a very familiar rear view.

Tallish. Lean.

Black overcoat. Black jeans.

"I guess I shouldn't have given you beer... Do I take you to the RSPCA to get your chip scanned...?"

My voice comes out quiet, dry and tired.

Jamie turns around with the most beautiful bunch of crazy-random coloured puppies in his hand.

Huh...?!

"I was just leaving these... thought you'd still be at work. I felt like such a bastard for not knowing it was your birthday."

"Who are you and what have you done with Jamie?... But seriously, why would you...?" I sigh.

"When's mine...?"

"November 6. You're a very naughty Scorpio."

"See...? Hey are you okay? You look shocking."

"Why thank you..."

Sarcasm. According to Shakespeare, the lowest form of wit...

"I've had a *very* bad day..."

With a *humph!* of a sigh, I reach around him to put my key in the door.

"...and I really just want to go to bed."

"I could help you with that..."

The faintest suggestion of *suggestive* in his voice.

"While we're getting your chip scanned, should we also get you neutered...?" I ask sweetly.

"You could hold the wake for it..."

"I don't think my apartment is big enough..."

He chuckles softly in my ear, and closing his hand over mine helps me turn the key.

"What are you doing?"

" I'm looking after you, if you'll let me."

"Who are you and what have you done with Jamie...?"

"I'm trying to be a Good Guy..."

"Not on my account, I hope."

He leads me to my room, sits me down on the bed, pulls my boots off, then raising my arms over my head like a toddler, gently pulls my jumper off.

And for once, looks at my eyes, not my black t-shirt bra.

"Do you have any useful tea?"

"I drink coffee. No tea is useful. Simon might..."

He disappears out to the kitchen. I unhook my bra, pull off my cargoes, then slip on the Nirvana t-shirt.

When I remember... *oh shit! Baby!*

I haven't checked my phone for hours.

Nope.

Still no baby.

I'm just about to slide into bed when he reappears with two steaming mugs. A faded Union Jack one and an even more faded I *Heart* New York one.

His jaw clenches.

"That's Josh's t-shirt."

I shrug, vaguely.

"I dunno... is it...?"

When we already know that I know it belonged to Josh Gillespie, who may or may not have been his best friend and with whom I may or may not found out that revenge is a dish best served naked.

He helps me into bed, fluffing the pillow that Mick put there just this morning (and how freaking weird is that...?)

This morning.

Which after everything I've been through feels like a lifetime ago.

I take a suspicious sip of the tea that smells like lemongrass, peppermint and eucalyptus. The usual weird sensation of hot, weak, flavoured water, but it doesn't taste too bad. Jamie kicks off his boots and sinks down next to me. On top of the covers.

"Want to talk about it...?"

"No. No I do not."

Quietly and emphatically.

And I'm pretty sure that if I do, I have to kill you.

And that's not in my skill set.

He turns to look at me intently.

"I know we never used to do much talking but..."

"I *really* don't want to talk about it"

Quietly, with a little shake of my head. From my hair to my toes, I am numb and I am completely whelmed. My brain is fried, and my body feels like it's attempted at least a few of the labours of Hercules. And even if I was at liberty to discuss this whole real-life horror movie with him... even if I actually *wanted* to open up to him... I have absolutely no idea where to begin to try to unpack it.

"I can't stop thinking about you. You used to be just a lovely little deer caught in headlights... When did you get so... *fierce...?*"

"London." My voice sounds small, flat and exhausted. It vaguely registers how offensive *just a lovely little deer* is, but I can't muster sufficient energy or care factor to set him straight.

"The Dull Duke?"

His voice tries a little too hard to sound casual.

"Nope. Sous-chef at a Michelin two-star restaurant. He teased me mercilessly 'til I could give as good as I got..."

I close my eyes as the corners of my mouth quite involuntarily start to curl up. His naked ass doing a Loser Lap of the pool table the first time we met... my naked ass on a cold, stainless steel commercial bench after-hours in his kitchen... Kissing in the middle of the road, in the rain, at 3am... How *doing* without thinking was the most insanely liberating thing...

"He was cheeky and naughty. It was fun... until he broke my heart..."

Dr Wolfe naturally makes it about Him and takes offence.

"Are you saying we *didn't* have fun?"

Oh God. I am too exhausted for this.

So the words just fall quietly out of my mouth.

"It felt like a four year audition for the role of Girlfriend... I kept getting call backs but you were never going to give me the part..." I mutter, smooshing down my pillow, preparing to bury my face in it. So exhausted and overwhelmed I'm seriously contemplating just closing my eyes, falling asleep and hoping he'll be gone when I open them, when-

"Sid! Sid! Where are you...?"

Footsteps on the wooden floor. Coming towards the door.

"You in here...?"

And there's Simon coming through the door... with a rapid-fire stream of consciousness coming straight out of his mouth. You get used to it...

"Oh hi Jamie! How are you? Facials tomorrow morning... I texted you like a million times but you didn't reply... Do you ever check your messages? That's why you're single - you know that, right...? In at ten, out by eleven thirty. Plenty of time to get to lunch with Delia, yes...?˙I called work but they said you'd gone home sick... You forgot the coffee, didn't you? I knew you would... *Oh!* You okay...?" He's just noticed I look like crap.

"Been better... been worse..." I murmur.

Shit! The coffee... I could tell you it's probably being processed as evidence on a psychopathic serial killer's little ship of horrors... but then I'd have to kill you...

Simon assesses the situation and takes charge. This is when I remember that making people compliant (sometimes against their will or better judgement) is an essential part of being a stylist. He points at me.

"Right! You! Sleeping. Now. And You-" he gestures to Jamie - "Leaving. Now."

I am very happy to do as I'm told. Given an essential part of being a surgeon is being treated like God, Jamie probably not so much...

I roll onto my side and snuggle under the covers. The mattress feels like a cloud as my exhausted and relieved body melts into it. Jamie may or may not whisper something in my ear as he kisses me softly on the cheek... I don't know and I don't care...

Because I'm going to be asleep in three... two... o-...

Ding!Ding!Ding!

My sleep... my beautiful, deep, restful, psychopath-free sleep... is interrupted by my phone. Hazily I look at the clock on the bedside table. It's 11pm.

Who the hell messages at eleven...?"

Oh shit!

Baby!!!

I grab my phone, look at the photo that's been sent and burst into tears. Two red-faced, dripping wet and kinda traumatised looking girls.

A baby girl!

Grace Violet.

Miranda and her new Mini Me.

I start typing...

Welcome to the world Gracie Violet! Yay You !!!

(with a truckload of love hearts)

Gran was - naturally! - right. Another Carlisle Girl...

I smile. God is in Her heaven, and all is well with the world.

My stomach rumbles like a volcano and I remember I haven't eaten since breakfast. Which seems like a lifetime ago...

I pad barefoot out to the kitchen (which wasn't the best idea, because it's fucking freezing...)

I make myself a very tasty ham sandwich and start stuffing it down as I trot back to bed. Glancing out the window, I notice something.

Perched high up on the bough of a naked tree... silhouetted by the moon...

Ravens!

Four to be precise.

Four for a birth...

Back in my bedroom, my gaze falls back on my phone.

Yep. There's really someone else I need to speak to...

I begin texting, but shake my head.

I tell Siri to make the call.

It's answered on the second ring.

"Hey."

The voice is pretty hostile. Short. Sharp. Guarded.

"Hey!" I reply with as much warmth as that one little syllable can hold.

"What...?"

Still on the offensive.

"Can I tell you something for nothing?"

"Nnnnn-noooo."

Sarcastically. But at least there's some kind of engagement with me.

"You deserve so much better than him. You are far too beautiful, too smart and too funny to ever be anyone's Plan B..."

And Lovely Larry can't quite hang up before a heartbreaking sob escapes her lovely lips. I shake my head and hope with all my heart she wakes up faster than I did...

Then I stretch and yawn... and snuggle down for some more beautiful, uneventful sleep.

Tuesday 9:00 am
Melbourne. Very Small Town.
How small...?
Let's find out, shall we...?

"Sid!... *Sid!... Cressida!!! Wake up!*"

Through the sweet fog of a completely uneventful night's sleep, I hear Simon. And I feel him shaking me.

"Mmmmmm..."

I slowly open my eyes to see his beautiful cornflower blue ones. And I can see in them the same relief that I'm feeling, because apart from being a little fuzzy around the edges, I feel perfectly normal.

"What's the time...?" I ask, trying to pull the day into focus.

"It's nine, Babe. Y'all better hustle if we're going to be on time for our spa appointment."

Mr Punctuality is - naturally! - already showered, dressed and looking clean, cool and well-moisturised. And he comes bearing a cup of coffee and a piece of Vegemite toast.

"Oh! I love you like a rainbow!" I say it and I mean it.

He is the best fairy godmother a girl can have.

Then I remember I have the best news ever.

"Hey Miranda had the baby!!! *A little girl!!!* Grace Violet."

"Fan-bloody-tastic! Little girls are *so* much more fun to dress... We can call in and see them tonight if she's up for it."

As I nod, he parks himself next to me on the bed. He's rocking a black t-shirt, chocolate grandpa cardigan, black jeans, snake print trainers and lots of silver jewellery.His face has turned an uncharacteristic shade of Serious.

"So..." he says emphatically. "Two things... The kidnapped girl thing. That's over now...?"

"Mmm-hmmm..."I nod vaguely with a mouthful of toast. Wish I could tell him everything, but I like him too much to kill him.

"Must be. Because she didn't come looking for me last night."

He nods and looks relieved. Then his brow furrows and he looks at me really hard.

"And the Jamie thing... What's happening with that...?"

"Don't worry..." I reach over and squeeze his skinny knee. "He's harmless. He's only chasing me because I have absolutely no interest in him. Ironic, much...?"

"Much! Now get in the shower Sleeping Beauty!"

He takes the empty coffee mug and plate from my hand and glances at the clock.

"C'mon Babe. You gotta hustle..."

I stand under the shower letting the blissfully hot water wash away the last three days. And the enormity of what happened finally starts to sink in. Because of me, a girl is alive. Because of me, she was spared a fate worse than death. I dreamt shit that actually happened. I assisted the Federal Police. Mick called me *his asset...*

I am quite possibly... *psychic...*

I need to talk to Gran about this... because I'm not so sure this is something I want to sign up for...

Because while I'm glad I helped save some girl, I don't know that I have room in my schedule or my head for something so consuming... and so freaking traumatic. However there's a lurking sense of something between Unsettled and Anxious that deep down, I know I don't actually have a choice.

Maybe it will never happen again.

Or maybe I get better at it.

Maybe it gets easier.

Simon has neatly laid out a tight black t-shirt, black yoga pants and my new grey cashmere hoodie. I stuff my feet into my

Birkenstocks (figuring I'm going to have to take everything off really soon anyway), screw my wet hair into a knot and grab my handbag.

I can't think of a better way to follow a whole night of beautiful, uneventful sleep, than lying like a rag doll while people do stuff to me for a little longer…

Melbourne. Small Town. Exhibit A.

If you don't know it's there, you probably won't find it... A discreet doorway in one of the little streets that run off a very busy main road. A panelled solid timber door in high gloss French navy. A satisfyingly heavy brass door handle and a tastefully small brass plate. *Entre Nous* is engraved in a very French, chic, cursive font. For those who were not subjected to learning French at school, it's pronounced *ontra noo* and it means 'between ourselves'... ie whatever witchcraft is worked to keep you from looking like the age on your Drivers Licence is strictly their little secret.

Our footsteps echo up two flights of dark wooden stairs that shine like a mirror. The walls are exactly the same moody violet-grey the sky turns just before an electrical storm.

We arrive at reception and the vibe is Stealth Wealth. Chandeliers, upholstered linen benches, gleaming glass and a little brass. Glamorous - but *very* tasteful.

Behind the counter is a girl, maybe a smidge taller than average and with a distinctly Paris vibe. Her glossy, dark hair is cut with heavy, blunt fringe and is pulled back into a perfect, jaunty ponytail. An angular, fox-like face with perfect eyebrows and plush eyelashes. Dark blue eyes, matt red lips. Her complexion is very youthful, but she has the poise of someone a little older and wiser.

She smiles warmly.

"Hello Simon! And you must be Cressida... Lovely to meet you! I'm Holly!" Her voice is almost child-like... light, enthusiastic and rather high in pitch.

"Please come through..."

She motions for us to follow her down a long, mood-lit hall-way, before stopping front of an almost invisible sliding door.

A small room.

Pristine white everything, softened with thoughtfully dimmed lighting.

"Cressida, you're in here with me...." She slides open an identical door directly opposite, revealing an identical white room, "...and Simon, you're in here. Claudia will be looking after you today."

Holly hands us white towelling wraps and leaves us with the instructions to take off everything except our knickers, looking directly at Simon as she says "including jewellery. *All the jewellery!*"

If Holly was a perfume, she would be top notes of Sweet, heart notes of Caring and bass notes of Bossy.

After doing as instructed, I climb up onto the white leather bed that runs diagonally across the room. As I sink into the plush towel that covers it, I realise *OMG!*. It's heated! Oh bliss! Ima think I could get used to being High Maintenance...

I'm staring at the ceiling (fresh and white, no cobwebs and strategically dotted with down lights) and listening to the muted French jazzy music that seems to be the soundtrack of the whole salon. There's a gentle knock at the door. Now I don't know about you, but I never quite know what I'm supposed to say. Somehow a squeaky little noise that sounds kind of like *okay* comes out of my mouth. Holly smiles warmly as she cocoons me in the softest, white fluffy blanket. I feel like a toddler being tucked into bed.

"Are you warm enough?" she asks, genuinely concerned. I notice she has the faintest dusting of freckles over the bridge of her nose. Her fingertips ever so gently touch my shoulders.

"So... close your eyes for me and we'll get started."

The lights get bright through my eyelids as her fingers move like tiny fairies over my face. Stretching the skin smooth, softly pinching it together here and there... as she asks many, many questions. The answer to most of which is No. Do I have a skincare regime? Do I drink eight glasses of water? Do I eat salmon and leafy greens? Do I limit my caffeine and alcohol? Do I cleanse my face every night? Do I use sunblock every day? Do I use eye cream? Do I use masks? Do I use serums? I explain that I use whatever Simon leaves in the bathroom, and with a pretty random frequency. I can feel one of her very perfect eyebrows raise.

"You're lucky. You're genetically blessed, you have your Mum's great skin - but that won't save you forever... You need to step up... now!... and I can help you with that."

So for the next ninety minutes, this is what happens... She announces what she's about to put on my face and what it's going to do for me. There's a succession of delicate-smelling potions - some cool and creamy, some warm and oily, some tingly to the point of discomfort - all applied with such a gentle, confident touch and calm, hypnotic rhythm that I... start to... melt into the bed... and slip away...

It's the same room, but it's different.

Still clean, crisp and comfortable, but less luxe. Holly is standing at the end of the bed, gently assessing a face I can't see.

"Hmmm... I know you mentioned Botox but I don't think you need it. Your face just needs some love. Let me do a light chemical peel and a massage. I can take five years off you just by getting you relaxed and hydrated."

"My wife is of the very strong opinion that 'we' would be happier if I have Botox..."

A man's voice. Deep, resonant but very controlled. Slightly self-mocking in tone and *sotto* in volume.

Oh God! I know that voice!
Argh!
It's on the tip of my tongue...
Who is it???

"I think your wife is wrong. These lines here... and here... give you character. They make you look distinguished. You've earned them. By taking better care of the rest of you, we can soften them."

"The rest of me...? What can you do with the rest of me?"

Is it just me, or has he just taken a very rapid turn for the Flirty...??? Which Holly pretends to ignore.

"The goal should be contentment, not happiness. Happiness is an emotion. It can only be transient. Contentment is a state of being that's sustainable."

"Who are you? Yoda with a ponytail...? Any more great wisdoms?"

"Yes. Stop opening your eyes or you'll get product in them!" as she laughs. An intoxicating, tinkling, childlike laugh.

"Can I see you again?" he asks very earnestly.

"Of course. I think I'm available same time, next week."

"That's not what I meant."

"Oh I know that's not what you meant."

"Where do you live, Holly?"

"Not telling."

"Okay... What's your surname, Holly?"

And then - *Boom!* - it hits me.

OMFG!!! That's Sebastian Marchesi.

And suddenly I know exactly what she's going to say next...

With a shuddering gasp I wake up. My eyes open wide and I look straight up through the blindingly bright light into Holly's very surprised face.

"You're Holly!"

Gently she pats my shoulders.

"Shhhhh. It's okay. You were in the deepest sleep. Just close your eyes and relax. Hang on, before you close let me just..."

Suddenly my eyeballs are stinging and I'm guessing I've got something in them not designed to go there. Holly delicately dabs them with cool water.

"There. Is that better?" She starts giggling. "And yes. I am very much Holly. Who else would I be...?"

And not just any Holly.

My pulse quickens and my mind starts spiralling out of control.

You're Seb Marchesi's mystery mistress.

You're Holly Golightly.

The Shiniest Unicorn in the Room.

"Oh thank God you're here!"

Libby looks like she's about to weep with joy as she reaches for the huge pile of Happy Baby orders for Miranda and Marco. Simon dropped me at work while he went to pick up some accessories for a shoot tomorrow. He looked me very sternly in the eye, while stabbing a finger at his smart watch and mouthing the words *one hour!*

"Any day without you isn't fun, but today is - oh! Look at you! All smooth and glowy and shiny! I remember the day spa..." And she looks so wistful and so very tired that I make a mental note to gift her some of my birthday present.

We spend what seems like forever sorting through the orders, prioritising some and saving others for when Miranda and baby Grace get sent home.

I do one from Mum, Dad and Larry - a really soft and pretty bouquet of roses in every shade of pink, with lime green viburnum foliage and a super-cute baby pink polka dot bow.

Then I go upstairs to the Goodie Room, which is floor-to-ceiling booze, chocolates... and plush toys.

"Hmmmm..." I scan a critical eye over the shelves of teddies, bunnies, monkeys... looking for... *omg!*...

THAT!

A fairy-soft white unicorn the size of a Labrador.

Perfect! Absolutely bloody perfect.

I wire together little bunches of violets and tie them together around her neck with a violet satin bow, like a garland on a prize show pony.

I take a few quick snaps of my handiwork and post with the usual business tags, plus #itsagirl #intstababy #tooprecious

Then I do a quick prowl around the shop, looking for something that looks like Gran... and... *Bingo!* Gorgeous purple dahlias - the same shade of amethyst as a Scottish thistle. I do a quick-but-pretty wrap job with dark green paper and matching ribbon.

Stop the clock!

"And Ima outta here!" I yell at the entire workroom. "See y'all tomorrow..."

Melbourne. Small Town. Exhibit B.

We jump out of Simon's car, simultaneously shuddering and muttering *Fark!!!* My grandparent's home backs onto the river and the wind blowing off it is arctic-cold. Under a bleak, grey sky, with teeth chattering, we crunch our way up the long, gravel path to Gran's front door. And as I start to lose feeling in my freezing toes, I'm really wishing I hadn't chosen my trusty Birkenstocks.

It's a large brick 1930's house.

Okay.

I guess technically it's a mansion... which has been modernised, but it hasn't been gutted and dragged into the 21st century like so many of the other grand old ladies in Toorak. The neat lawn is strewn with petals - the last of Gran's roses have been collateral damage of the wind.

Before I can ring the doorbell, Gran flings the door open and grabs my face in her hands, planting the biggest, smoochiest kiss on my lips... and I know that she knows.

"I'm so very proud! I always knew it would come back to you!" she beams at me. I just shrug. I really don't know what to say.

"I didn't really *do* anything... I just kinda had a few nightmares..."

"You saved a girl's life, Dear!"

"Well... yes... but I can't say it was much fun... One star. Would not recommend..."

"It gets easier..." Her face clouds with concern. "Did it knock you about a bit...?"

"The first one was a shocker. Like the hangover from hell and food poisoning rolled into one...I felt like I'd been hit by a truck all day... then the last one I actually *had* the hangover from hell on top of the rollercoaster of psychic angst..." I giggle. "I guess the others weren't quite as bad... on hang on! That wasn't the last one... I just had another one..."

And that was just like waking up from a strange dream. Omg - I can't believe I know who Holly is, and I'm dying to tell Simon... but in the spirit of Entre Nous (not to mention the terrifying power of Seb Marchesi...) I don't know that it's my secret to tell.

Gran is grinning from ear to ear.

"So you're starting to pick up on things...? Things just... *present themselves*... somewhere between your conscious and unconscious minds...? *Oh! Excellent!*"

274

We've walked down the hall... past the formal lounge to the left and dining room on the right... past grandpa's study... and arrived at the kitchen and family room.

The whole back wall is glass. Not clean, modern glass but French doors and windows with small, rectangular panes, all painted crisp white.

And the crazy barking starts, as Otis and Minka - Gran's two black Standard Poodles - see us.

"Poo-doools!!!" I yell at them, suddenly so very happy to see their smiling faces and wagging tails as I open the door for them.

And they're beside themselves to see us too!

We're smothered in Poodle Joy as they throw themselves at us, bouncing on their hind legs like kangaroos, trying to plant kisses on our faces. These are not neurotic handbag accessories with weird haircuts. These are Dobermanns with afros. Gran doesn't have the 'puffy bits' on them - she gets them clipped short all over, so they just look like regular dogs.

"Where's my Best Boy...?!"

Otis has wrapped his front feet around my neck. I bend down to hug my arms around his ribcage and plant a *Mwah!* on his long, velvety snout.

Minka is nibbling Simon's arm with her tiny front teeth.

"Ouch! I don't have fleas!"

Mouth wide open - which makes her look somewhat unhinged - she looks at Simon triumphantly as if to say *Well you don't now!*

"There's champagne in the fridge, if you'd be so kind as to open it Simon, Dear. I thought I'd make us a nice paella for - "

And the doorbell rings.

I exchange a suspicious glance with Simon. We weren't expecting anyone else, were we...?

The Poodles charge down the hall, barking their heads off in Crazy Guard Dog Mode.

"Oh... could you please get that Dear...?" Grandma says, possibly a little too casually.

Poodles escort me to the front door, their big, resonant barks reverberating from the polished floorboards up to echo throughout the high ceiling - and make my eye twitch.

"Hey! C'mon... get back!" I attempt to control the crazed Poodles as I open the door...

And standing there is a rugged blond man.

Shearling lined jacket over broad shoulders, well-loved yet ironed jeans, black thermal t-shirt. And eyes every colour of the ocean.

Secret Agent Mick...?

My brain spins, trying to contextualise.

Oh! He must need to ask me some more questions...

Hang on! I'm at Gran's...

How the hell would he know I'm here...?

And then I notice Otis and Minka have switched from ferocious to friend mode, their tails wagging like crazy.

His smile is equal parts smug and awkward.

"Hey Big Guy!" as he tousles the curls on Otis' head, while Minka rubs and twerks around his legs like an exotic dancer.

So...

I wrinkle my nose in astonishment, disbelief and discomfort.

Well... this is a little bit unexpected and a whole lot weird.

"Action Man...?!"

"Rich Girl."

Yup. Gran's Michael From The Country is... *our* Secret Agent Mick...

Melbourne is a ridiculously small town.

"Michael, dear!"

Gran appears behind me, wiping her hands on a tea towel. He bends down and kisses her on the cheek.

Seriously? You're on Kissing Terms...?

I notice he's holding a small package of newspaper, which he presents to her.

"Mum thought you might like these... I think she said Bearded Iris...? Does that make sense? She said to put them in the ground now..."

"Oh! Lovely! Do tell her I said thank you... Now... Finally!... Cressida, this is Michael. Michael, this is Cressida - although fate may have beaten me to it ..." she grins. Very well-pleased with herself.

He looks me right in the eye, and my breath catches in my throat... which is quite ridiculous, because he is *so* not my type.

He holds out his hand and smiles a little sheepishly.

"Pleased to meet you Cressida."

"Oh no! The pleasure is entirely mine, Michael."

And he takes my hand in mock formality...

And... *Ouch!* There's that spark again.

"Could you stop electrocuting me?!"

"Maybe *you're* the one electrocuting *me*, Rich Girl... Ever think about that?"

"Oh don't be ridiculous!"

Well, at least the Poodles are happy to see him, doing their crazy leaping and 360 degree spinning Happy Dance as they lead him to the kitchen.

Gran takes in Mick's rear view.

"Look at that bum! Don't you just want to - "

"Gran! Behave!" I hiss under my breath in a horrified whisper.

"Never, Child. Never!" she replies with a saucy wink.

Great... To this ocean of weird, we can now add a Naughty Nana.

Simon looks up from the three glasses of freshly fizzing Champagne, blinking in confusion. I bring him up to speed.

"So... as it would happen... Grandma's Michael and Special Agent Mick are indeed the same person."

The blinking continues, and his jaw drops open.

"*Fark me!* Melbourne is a small town!" shaking his head as he reaches up to grab a fourth champagne flute.

"Not for me, thanks Mate. I'm working this arvo."

He gets himself a glass, goes to the fridge and pours himself some of Gran's homemade kombucha. With ice.

I frown a little bit, not quite knowing what to make of a strange man making himself at home in my Grandma's kitchen.

Gran raises her glass.

"To good health and good friends!... And to Cressida's Spiritual Awakening! It truly is a marvellous thing!"

Spritual awakening sounds so New Age wanky it makes me wince.

"Actually it was a pretty rude awakening and I'm not so sure *marvellous* would be my adjective of choice..."

"You've been ignoring it for twenty years. Saturn had to get your attention."

I wrinkle my nose at her, then turn to Mick.

"You working *again*...? Don't you get some time off after -" I stop myself mid-sentence. *Shit!* I can't say any more. Luckily he smoothly picks up my dropped ball.

"Only the crims get time off for good behaviour. Something has to be delivered in person and I drew the short straw. I fly out tonight."

"Oh..."

And it's out of my mouth before I can stop it. One little syllable that gives away far too much - confusion, fear, worry. Secretly I'd been hoping that He hadn't survived the raid... that they'd all been shot dead... I shudder involuntarily. Simon doesn't miss it - he never misses anything. Fortunately Gran is oblivious, her head bent over the paella pan.

"Now, Dear, I'm going to need some parsley from the garden for my sofrito. And a couple of lemons..."

Now... call me crazy, but I assume she's talking to me... however Mick and I both put down our glasses and simultaneously head to the back door.

I must be giving him a strange look, because as we cross the patio he says -

"Is this weird...?"

"What? You, hanging with my Gran...? *What could possibly be weird about that???*" I think it comes out of my mouth a little louder than intended.

Poodles lead the way past the pool to the big, rambling garden beyond. Otis brings Mick a tennis ball, which he gently takes from his mouth, then throws. One of those effortless, competent masculine throws. Unlike my throws, which are sad, disappointing and give girls who throw balls a bad name.

Otis and Mink fly off after the ball and he turns his attention to me.

"Your gran is an amazing lady and I enjoy spending time with her. My mum is three hours away..." he frowns slightly and his face softens. "I'm very close to her and I miss her. Delia is a bit of a substitute mum for me -"

He chuckles, a little bashfully.

"- and I help out around here. Your family is a little short on Useful Men Folk... she gets me to do all the things Laurie shouldn't be doing at his age - like anything that involves ladders, heavy lifting or chainsaws."

I nod. Slowly and thoughtfully. His face looks completely different when he's not in Action Man mode. I raise an eyebrow at him.

"So... you're not just a pretty face either..."

He shakes his head and laughs. An easy, musical laugh. A fleeting glimpse of authentic Michael without the tough guy veneer. Human. Almost vulnerable. Relaxed and unguarded, his face looks... handsome...???

As we head toward the little orchard of fruit trees, I can't help but notice that we've fallen perfectly in step with each other. A raven descends, on a mission to snaffle the last fig on the almost naked tree. But the branch is too slender for his chunky body and he quickly finds himself upside down as it bends dramatically under his weight.

One for sorrow...

Then I remember the unpleasant little thing that's been knocking at my brain.

"So... what happened to... *him*...?"An involuntary shudder goes through my body as I remember the cold, reptilian eyes I've been trying so hard to forget.

"There were gunshots...?" my voice rises hopefully. I can't help it. I hope he's dead.

"They were all taken alive. Our Soggys are too good for accidents-"

"*Soggys...?*"

"The big guys in black. Special Operations Group... He's being extradited. Tonight. I drew the short straw."

"Wh-"

"Don't ask that. You know I can't tell you where."

"Somewhere he can't buy his way out...?"

"God I hope so."

We've reached the lemon tree and I pause, about to begin the climb up the middle of it to get the really good ones at the top.

"Hey! Should you really be doing that...? In highly inappropriate footwear? I can reach one."

"Bah! Been doing this for years. Those ones right up there are better."

And up I go... although I have to say it was easier when I was eight... and these bloody Birkenstocks aren't helping.

I grab two perfectly golden-ripe ones, then begin my one-handed descent... which isn't going too badly til my shoe gets stuck in a gnarly branch and I lose my balance. His hands are around my ribcage in a split second.

"It's okay. I'm fine." I recover, but those hands are still there.

"No. I'm helping you down. I'm not telling Delia you fell out of a tree on my watch."

I sigh in frustration as I drop the lemons to the ground and place my hands on his shoulders.

Mmmmm... Hard! My brain may find him irritating, but my body would strongly argue that he has potential.

He pauses, looking up at me. I do swear he's trying hard not to smirk.

"Could you please just put me down...?"

"Could you please just let me help you...?"

Could he be any more irritating...?

No. He could not.

"Have you ever thought about seeking help for this Hero Complex...?"

"Have you ever thought about doing as you're told...?"

"Hmmm... can't say it's ever crossed my mind..."

Finally he lifts me out of the tree, placing me carefully on the ground. But he's still not letting go. He looks into my eyes. He's serious.

"Well I need you to start. If things had gone pear-shaped yesterday, right now I'd be trying to explain to Delia how I lost you. Did you think of that...? This is not a game - it's real. It could have ended very... *badly*..."

His voice trails off and he shakes his head. Too disturbing for words. I turn my head to avoid his gaze, knowing he is - once again - right.

I'm debating whether to justify, apologise or change the subject when he turns abruptly, stalking off to the herb garden.

He bends over a lush, green plant and starts grabbing handfuls.

"Errr... watcha doin'...?" I ask cautiously.

"Delia asked for parsley. Remember...?" he replies. Smugly.

"Except that's not parsley. That's coriander..."

Whoever said Being Kind is More Important than Being Right clearly has never met Action Man...

So lunch is surprisingly pleasant. Gran's paella is sensational. Conversation is never going to be dull when Simon's at the table. And Mick becomes much more entertaining when he's not saving the world and taking himself too seriously. Gran watches us like a hawk, looking for the faintest glimmer of attraction.

'So... I'm trapped in this hotel suite pretending to be a masseuse... working out if I can pluck a hair somewhere from this gangster's body without him noticing, because his DNA would be really handy... when...” he pauses for effect, his eyes twinkling and the corners of his mouth starting to curl up. “When he rolls over and asks me if I do Happy Endings!”

Simon splutters a mouthful of champagne over the table, while Gran and I throw our heads back and laugh out loud.

“So did you get that cool scar in a knife fight or something exciting???” Simon asks, intrigued by the Action Man. Mick's fingers go absently to his left cheek.

“Nah Mate... Got it at school.”

“Ooooh! Were you fighting over a girl...? How romantic...”

“Nup. I was fighting over a football. We won the Premiership by two points.”

"Mmmm... You've got this effortless-rugged-masculine thing going on... I really like your look, Mick!"

"Errrr... thank you... " is Mick's very uncomfortable reply to Simon.

"Oh! Oh! *Oh!!!*" Simon has a Lightbulb moment. He has them often. You'll get used to it. "I need a guy for a photo shoot... Old school Aussie, blokey, footy captain type...You'd be perfect!"

"Yeah-nah Mate. Hard pass from me."

Yeah-nah in this context means *Not happening - that is a really fucking bad idea.* Simon is not perturbed. He hears No quite frequently in his line of work and always interprets it as a sign to try a different angle.

"Oh well... there's plenty of time for you to think about it... it's not for a few weeks yet..."

"No. Not happening."

"It'd be the easiest thousand bucks you ever make... and the catering will be fabulous... and you'll get to keep everything you wear..."

Mick shakes his head, but you can see a flicker in his eyes that Food, Money and Free Stuff may have been the right carrots to dangle.

He glances at his watch and pushes his chair back from the table.

"I better make a move. Thanks for lunch, Delia."

"Mmmm... We better hustle too, Sid."

"What are you two up to...? Going to see my beautiful granddaughter...?"

"Yes... right after Cressida poses topless for a life-size mural of the Karma Sutra..."

Gran blinks. Looks surprised... then confused... then she starts laughing. Really, really laughing. Like tears running down her cheeks.

"Oh you're a trick, Simon! How funny! Karma Sutra indeed!"

However the Effective Detective noticed the alarmed glance I shot Simon and how I watched Gran's reaction a little too intently. And for a split second he drops his game face, looking equal parts bewildered and intrigued.

"Isn't he just *hilarious*!" I mutter through clenched teeth, giving Simon a stealthy (yet violent) punch in the arm as we walk up the hall to the front door.

Mick bends down to kiss Gran on the cheek, then extends his hand to Simon... who disregards it and throws his arms around him. Simon is a Hugger. From the look on Mick's face, Mick not so much.

Gran gives me a huge hug.

"Oh Trouble! I'm so very proud of you! Take care of yourself, Dear."

"Trouble...?" Mick is intrigued.

"We've called her that since she was a bairn... Not that she was ever *bad*, mind you... she was just always a little *creative*..."

And then Mick is turning to look at me. (Oh! And *bairn* is Scottish for baby...)

"*TROUBLE!*" as he nods, smiling a little too gleefully.

"Don't even think about it!" I waggle a finger of warning at him. "You do not have the right to call me *Trouble*... even if I *was*... and anyway, I am not... I'm just *creative*. You heard the Lady."

"You are a visual representation of Trouble... Try to keep out of trouble, Trouble."

"You seriously want to go there...?"

"Okay then... *Rich Girl* it is!" His eyes do a quick - yet pointed - lap of the grand house facade and the grand front garden. His mouth is smirking. "You going to try to argue *Rich Girl*, because seriously you got nothing... Try to stay out of trouble, Rich Girl."

"Try not to be an asshole, Action Man."

Could he be any more irritating...?

No. He could not.

"Pool. Same time, same place?"

Oh golly! Saturday night seems like a lifetime ago. So he was serious about that...? It was fun and, hell, no one else ever wants to play pool with me...

"Hmmm... I think so. I'll leave a message with Costa if I can't make it."

"Or you could just text me. You have my number."

"I *could*, but I'm not going to."

"Are you always so difficult...?"

"Are you always so bossy...?"

Gran and Simon have been following our to-and-fro like they're watching a tennis game. And then I remember the unpleasant task Mick has in front of him.

"Hey... good luck with the... " my voice trails off, and I wonder if my eyes can adequately convey the swirling mess of emotions that resurfaced the second I let myself think about Him and everything he's done. I guess I must have come pretty close, because Mick's face softens. He gives my hand a quick, gentle squeeze.

"Cheers! It'll be okay. You're okay? Yes...?"

I look up into his eyes and pressing my lips together, nod very slowly.

"Yep. I'm pretty sure I am."

And we're sitting in Simon's car under the grey Melbourne sky, the wind blowing autumn leaves all around us, driving along the murky, brown river towards the city that seems to spring up out of nowhere on the opposite bank, like a film set. I crank the seat-warmer up to max and snuggle back into the smooth, toasty leather.

The back seat is covered with bags from designer baby boutiques. Looks like Gracie has got herself a fairy godmother too...

"Can I just say my God he's hot and my God you make the cutest couple...?"

"No and no. I am not remotely interested."

"Hashtag givemickachance."

"Hashtag idrathereatglass... Not happening... like trying to bring back sayin' *hashtag*... that's not happening either, Babe."

"And yet I just made you do it.... *So...*" Simon's customary way of indicating a Change of Subject, as the car glides into an inner-city parking spot that has magically appeared. "Ready Freddie...?"

And suddenly a little wave of panic breaks over me.

No.

No I am not ready.

I bite my lip and glance furtively down at the car door handle. To quote Miranda... *This is a really bad idea...* Perhaps I should ask Simon to call and say I'm sick...? Perhaps I shouldn't involve Mojitos in decision-making processes that require full-frontal nudity...?

I do not know what the hell happened After Midnight, but my previously pretty normal little life seems to have become one weird, random and ridiculous adventure after another since I turned twenty-seven...

So why stop now...?

"Let's do this!"

Tuesday 4:00pm
Melbourne. Small town.
Exhibit C.

Down a little city street... turn up the bluestone laneway where the cult croissant shop with the queue halfway down the street is on the corner... and there it is.

In amongst the historic red brick walls is a door painted bright magenta, with hand painted, shiny black letters that read Sweat Equity.

I take a deep breath and slowly reach up to press the security buzzer.

"Want me to come up with you?" Simon asks like he's a parent taking me to a dental appointment.

And like a kid with a date with the dentist, I press my lips together and nod. Wide-eyed and silent.

Two flights of stairs later, a huge wall of mirror surrounded by exercise machines, benches, kettle bells and racks of weights comes into view. The gigantic loft space is part gym, and part the very funky residence Diego and Jess call home. She appears, looking every inch the spectacular Amazon, in leopard print gym tights and a tiny black t-shirt with #liftlikeagirl emblazoned on her fabulous chest.

"Right on time! Ready to make the Karmageddon Wall of Fame...?" she says with a grin.

Ready...?

Ready is a very big word, but what the hell... let's just get it over with...

"We'll be with you in a few minutes - just working on some sexy arms'n'pecs for you - *hey! I saw that!* Half reps don't count. You wanna do another twenty...?"

And we notice a guy wearing basketball shorts (and nothing but basketball shorts...) lying face up on a bench with an impossibly large dumbbell in each hand. With a ripple of those ridiculous abs, in one effortless movement he raises himself to vertical.

And that's when I notice his eyes.

Kind, brown and twinkling.

With criminally long, thick lashes.

Somehow familiar, but how...???

Did he just wink...? Or did I imagine that...?

Jess makes the introductions.

"Cressida meet Lachlan. Lachlan meet Cressida. Hey... do you two know each other...?" Jess is looking a tad confused.

He holds my gaze. Carefully.

Oh!

Just like a real-life superhero...

He wears a mask. He has a nickname. His true identity is protected.

"I don't think so... He looks a bit like someone I met on a boat once..."

"Oh those booze cruises can end very badly..." Simon chimes in, speaking from experience.

"Mmmmm... If you're not careful they can be... *deadly*... even..." Lachlan is smiling but his unwaveringly direct eye contact leaves no doubt at all of two things.

That he is indeed my mystery man-in-black hero, Tex... and that Melbourne is... indeed... a very... *very*... small town.

BEAUTY SLEEP

Cressida Carlisle Mystery Number Two

What happens next...???

Here's a sneak peek!

Friday 3.08pm

Accidents WILL Happen.

"Hell-ooo-ooo...?" I call out hopefully into the vast, darkened and deserted space.

Is there anything more desolate than a nightclub in the cold, hard light of day...? No. There is not.

Technically Chou-Chou is a Gentleman's Club. The podiums and poles strategically placed amongst the tables and plush chairs give the game away. However this isn't just any titty bar. This an exclusive club where men of *very* highly disposable incomes (both legally earned and ill-gotten) come to do business and ogle the girls who work here (who are prettier, more talented and better paid than your average stripper.)

Hmmm. No cleaners. No staff.

I head towards the discreet door next to the bar which is marked 'Private'. It opens onto a corridor of identical doors - all closed except for the one furthest away which is slightly ajar. Two male voices drift out into the hallway. As I slowly and quietly walk towards it, I can make out words.

"Divorce is not an option. It'll be too expensive and she'll turn it into a media circus."

"Mmmmm. Bad for business. Bad for bank account."

"And bad for my kids..." His voice becomes impassioned.

"Then you need *accident*..."

I stop dead in my tracks and my hand involuntarily rises to stifle the gasp that almost escapes my lips. Seb Marchesi is about to plan the murder of his wife.

I sneak a little closer, so I don't miss anything. I can see the corner of his desk on the facing wall. Lying in front of it, with his powerful jaw resting on his elegantly crossed paws, is Nero. His Dobermann.

He sees me. His eyes light up and I know he's about to spring to his feet.

300

"Ssshhh!" I motion almost silently, softly holding a finger to my lips. Then I hold up two fingers. "Just give me two seconds, okay...?"

He exhales theatrically as he sinks back down to the ground.

"Are we boring you, Nero?" asks Marchesi.

"Pity she doesn't have serious illness..." the other voice has a faint slavic accent.

"Oh... she has a heart condition..."

"She has a heart...?"

Both men laugh. I stifle a giggle too. Given what that woman has put me through so far today, you really can't blame me.

"She has a heart murmur. And a dependence on phentermine and fenfluramine."

"Diet pills? Could cause heart attack. Probably... mmmmm... yes. But can't say *when*..."

"Exactly. I can't be implicated but I need a more solid deadline. No pun intended."

They both chuckle.

"There is new guy. Serb. Ex-military. He specialise in car accident. Road to beach house on cliff *very windy... very dangerous....*"

"Absolutely not. She never goes to the beach without the kids. It would need to be-"

I'm sorry but I can't listen to any more. And I'm chicken that I'm going to get busted eavesdropping. I take a deep breath and knock briskly on the doorframe.

"Mr Marchesi...? Hello...?" I call out, hoping my voice sounds chirpy and innocent.

There's a beat of silence before Nero crosses the room in a single bound and flicks the door wide open with his nose. I enter the room, with the huge vase of fifty offending roses balanced on my hip like a toddler and Nero dolphin-flicking my free hand with his muzzle, trying to make me pat him.

Seb Marchesi is reclined in the chair behind his desk. His long, muscular legs are stretched out languidly in front of him, his feet (in his very expensive shoes) rest next to his wireless keyboard.

"Ah... Miss Carlisle..." his manner is light and casual, but for a split second his eyes are dark and intense as they scan my face for any sign that I overheard something I should not have.

"My wife..." - he continues lightly, whilst looking me right in the eye - "... couldn't you just murder her...?"

www.ingramcontent.com/pod-product-compliance
Lightning Source LLC
Chambersburg PA
CBHW051410170626
46809CB00006B/2093